For S ♡ ‖‖‖‖‖‖‖‖‖‖‖‖‖‖‖‖‖‖ **W9-BZB-534**

ANINDITA

DAUGHTERS OF PAPUA

Dear Sue,
Thank you for all your
supports!

Stefanny Irawan
Oct 2, 2015

Dalang Publishing

dp

Indonesian Literature

Lian Gouw

dalangpublishing@gmail.com
www.dalangpublishing.com

2014 Map of Indonesia

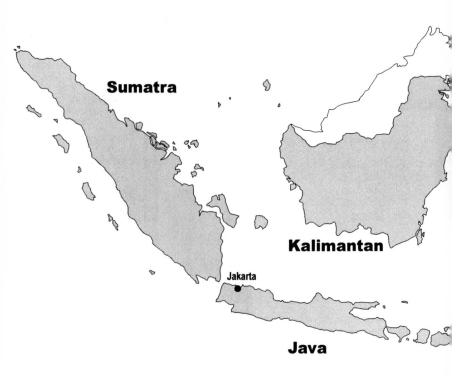

Sumatra

Kalimantan

Jakarta

Java

Indian Ocean

Pacific Ocean

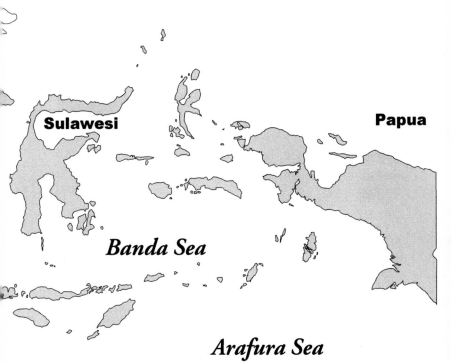

Sulawesi

Papua

Banda Sea

Arafura Sea

Map of Papua

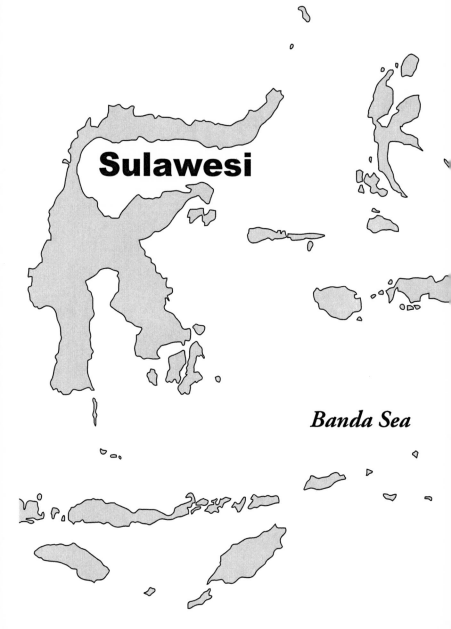

Sulawesi

Banda Sea

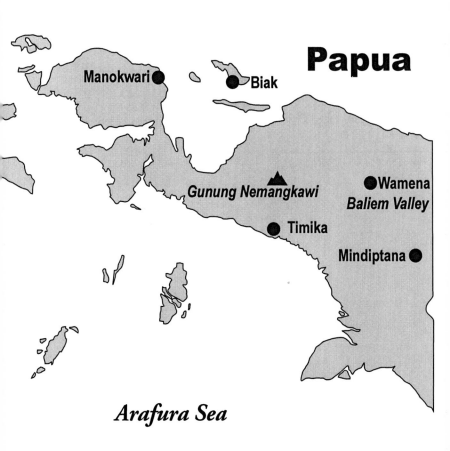

Daughters of Papua

Anindita Siswanto Thayf
Translated from the Indonesian
by Stefanny Irawan

dp Dalang Publishing

Daughters of Papua
Originally published as *Tanah Tabu* in 2009 by Penerbit PT Gramedia
Pustaka Utama, Jakarta, Indonesia (ISBN: 978-979-22-4567-7)
Copyright © 2009 Anindita Siswanto Thayf
Translation copyright © 2014 Stefanny Irawan

*Publication of this book is subsidized by the Center for Research and
Development, Office of Research and Development, Ministry of
Education and Culture of the Republic of Indonesia, and in collaboration
with Penerbit PT Gramedia Pustaka Utama.*

Cover design: Herfitrisna Yulianti Asnar
Book design: Son Do
Editor: Sal Glynn
Indonesian literary advisors: Manneke Budiman and
                                Purwanti Kusumaningtyas

Dalang Publishing LLC
San Mateo, CA
www.dalangpublishing.com
dalangpublishing@gmail.com

ISBN: 978-0-9836273-9-5
Library of Congress number: 2014950782

DAUGHTERS OF PAPUA

Translator's Note

Daughters of Papua occupies a special place in my life as a reader and a translator. The novel is an important work in Indonesian contemporary literature that directs the spotlight to the farthest east region of Indonesia. Anindita Siswanto Thayf provides a rare glimpse of Papua's people and culture. She gives voices to the important issues on the island that normally fall through the cracks of mainstream news media, issues like social welfare, education, domestic violence, and politics. Anindita does this through the three female characters encompassing different generations: a wise and tough grandma, a single mother with a dark past, and a smart, inquisitive little girl. The under-represented population of the society is given center stage in her story. Pum and Kwee, a dog and a pig, are more than mere narrators. Their unique insights are critical commentaries on the issues facing the women. *Daughters of Papua* serves as an eye-opening representation of Papua in Indonesian literature.

Daughters of Papua flexed my translation muscles, perhaps more than ever. Anindita's novel compelled me to learn more about my own language, particularly about the nuance and color, I had to preserve and carry into the translation. Discussing my work with Dalang Publishing's two beyond-wonderful editors, Lian Gouw and Sal Glynn, enabled me to learn so much about creating a quality translation. In the end, it was worth every moment.

Stefanny Irawan
July 2014

DAUGHTERS OF PAPUA

Here is resistance at the end of patience
Doom at the edge of desire
And tears are only for the frail ones

Chapter 1

PUM

(Timika, 2003) The sun is still rising in the sky, yet the heat is already scorching. It forces my pores to open wide and produce droplets of sweat the size of rice grains that dampen every fold of my skin. When the heat is this intense, a dog like me only needs a breeze to be comfortable. People seek shelter in their houses and under their fans. I stay on the porch and let the breeze tickle through my fur until I become part of burning nature, and my sweat and odor evaporate. Really, I am most comfortable when I am stretched out lazily with my ear flaps floppy and all. I relax as the hot day turns to noon. The usual noon, the noon I like.

Noon is heavenly because everything springs to life. The trees seem taller and make bigger patches of shade, clouds decorate the sky, the village gets busy, and clothes fresh from washing hang outside. This last one is my favorite: I love noon best for the filled clotheslines. I enjoy the pungent odors that come from vibrant colors of the wet clothes hanging on those lines in front of the mamas' houses or flung across the fence.

The different scents represent the colors Mabel knows by name: tranquil green forest under a bright blue sky; yellow bird-of-paradise and red-crested cockatoo; purple-stemmed *keris* plants, yellow-finned *arowana*, black orchids, giant red fruits; and even a congregation of crocodiles are made charming by their emerald glow. Everything grows in the wilderness. Everything is so fresh, so full of charm and vitality.

When I was a puppy, I believed I lived in a secret paradise. An untouched sacred land. I was lucky to grow up here.

Once I thought the beauty would last forever, protected by the love and gratitude for God's greatness by the simple and humble dreams of living. But I was wrong. I was so wrong. Life has taught me how extreme beauty is like a piece of raw meat that attracts hungry predators. It never fails to excite the greed of people and their desire to own and control. They take it little by little for themselves. They refuse to share.

A hunter I know once said, "Life is cruel, my brother. You need to be cruel to survive."

From then on, I understood why tribes wage wars and why immigrants take things away—just like every hunting dog must sink its teeth without mercy into its victim's flesh and disregard the heartbreaking cry. Still, I have kept hope inside, a hope that has lately been resurfacing. What if, one day, life stops being cruel? Will dogs and people no longer need to be cruel? I hope so. I mean, I am too old to be as cruel as I used to be, and too old to fight against the cruelty of others. I want to live the rest of my time peacefully, surrounded by the things that make me feel good and warm, like in this colorful, long-gone piece of heaven.

The smell of colors brings back the heartwarming memories, the colors that present themselves on the clotheslines, dancing in front of me. As I pay more attention to them, the colors fade because of cheap detergent, sweat, and weather. What a sorry situation.

This throws me back to today and lessens my hope. What is gone will never return, although some of those who stole promised to give it back. Like a bone with the meat stripped away. Can meat grow back on a bare bone?

Saddened, my eyes ran back to the clothes. Mama Helga's clothes. They are my favorite for their scent. But wait a moment; something is missing. Her fading yellow tee shirt with a tree printed on it is nowhere to be seen. Now that I think of it, it has been gone for quite a while. The tee shirt was a giveaway and everyone in the village has one. What sets hers apart is the fact that she still wears it even though it has been ten years, when I was a much younger dog. She brought it home from the festival on the soccer field. Other people had stopped wearing the yellow tee shirts and exchanged them with red, green, or even blue ones, and lately there is even a pink one. Ugh, I don't like the pink one. It reminds me of the spit from those who chew and suck on *pinang*—a mix of areca nut, betel leaf, and *gambir*. The spit is everywhere on the street.

I like the smell of yellow because it grabs my attention and reminds me of how clever they are for choosing it as the dominant color of their party flag. It reminds me of the sun, chicks, and dandelions.

Oh, we were talking about Mama Helga's tee shirt. I wonder what happened to it. Did someone steal it? I wonder for only a short time. The answer comes when I hear her yelling from inside the house.

"Yosi, do not use that to clean your brother's pee. Use this cloth instead."

The tee shirt with a tree print had turned into a dirty rag under Yosi's small foot, and soaked up the puddle of her baby brother's urine on the floor.

I yawn. Nothing lasts in this world, including the color yellow.

The sun moves steadily higher. Soon, she will start her journey home and it will be time for a nap. I am waiting.

KWEE

Never compare me to the lazy old dog in front of the house. I am not like him. Pigs have clean bristles instead of dirty fur, hooves instead of those weak pads dogs are stuck with, and are much more handsome. At this time of day, a pig like me prefers to be on his feet, moving around the house and the yard, and sometimes visiting Mabel in the kitchen.

"Shoo. Go away. Just play outside. Don't bother me here," she says, waving her hand. She also sends a certain delicious smell my way, a smell that naturally calls for me to come closer. Hmm... I know what she is making for the day.

"We are going to have the papaya-leaf dish. You like it, right?" she says without looking at me. I let out a happy squeal and move away. I never want to make her angry. Not once. She is always nice and kind, treating me like her own offspring.

Mabel is her nickname, from Mama Annabel, which is a mouthful when you need to shout it. Like other mamas, Mabel is old. Her age shows in her graying hair, and her loose skin looks like a wrinkled sheet here and there. But never underestimate Mabel's strength. Her big hands can easily grab a hold of your neck and snap it. Her big body has no difficulty hiding two little kids behind her. This is true. I saw it happen a few months ago.

Mabel was dealing with a drunken *paitua* who was trying to abuse his children. Those poor kids were running away from their father, crying so hard that tears streamed down their cheeks. They ran toward Mabel as she swept the yard. She hid them behind her back as he chased after them.

That drunken man tried to reach over Mabel's mountain-like body and grab his kids but without success. No matter how many times he tried, he failed. It was like trying to throw your arms over a gate which was simply too large for you.

At one point, the paitua got angry and decided to teach Mabel a lesson. Taking a few steps back, he launched himself full force at Mabel's puffed and proud chest. It may be hard to believe, but he ended up unconscious on the ground and the kids spend the rest of the morning in peace.

When angry, Mabel will turn into a fierce giant with nostrils the size of a well that can suck you in with one inhale. But you don't have to worry. My Mabel only gets angry for a reason. I mean, she always directs her anger to the right target.

Besides Mabel, two other residents of this house care about me and never treat me wrong. The first one is a young woman called *Mace*. She is younger than Mabel, but already has deep lines on her forehead, like those on a tree trunk made by a machete, making her look almost as old as Mabel and the other mamas. Luckily, her hair is still black and her breasts are firm enough to attract some glances from the men. Too bad the rest of her body does not share the same trait. Her body is thin and withered. Her eyes have lost their shine. She looks like an empty and drying sago palm tree. Unattractive. It repels love and money, say the gossipy mamas at the end of the street. A sign of infertility says the young, unemployed man at the neighborhood watch post. I, of course, reject all those comments because they really do not know that my sweet Mace is full of compassion.

Since I was little, Mace has taken care of me. She treats me like she treats Leksi, her own daughter. I eat what Leksi eats. She cradles Leksi in her arms while she pets me. When she takes Leksi for a walk, she brings me along. Her thin body is not caused by lack of eating. Mabel does not eat much either, but her body stays big. Mace is thin because she has a lot on her mind. I often find her crying quietly by the well at the back of the house or in the middle of the field. She never cries inside the house, and if you ask Mabel, you will get different answers. Why? Because Mabel has her own answers, and her own ways that make her different from other mamas in this village.

Leksi is older than me by a few years and I love her. But I do not call her sweet because she is like a sister to me. I call her so because every time she smiles, two dimples emerge on her cheeks. She is also agile like a *karaka*, escaping children's hands when they try to catch it. She always jumps around, runs, climbs, and does whatever she likes except standing still or staying put. Ah, Leksi. I suddenly miss her and get impatient to see her again. I want to play the fun game we played yesterday.

Unfortunately, my dear Leksi is at school. Lately I feel that we have been separated on purpose although it only happens from morning to noon. We used to be together all the time, wherever and whenever. Can I go to school, too?

"The teacher and headmaster at school get angry and punish whoever does not follow the rules, Kwee," Leksi said when she saw me trying to follow her to school. At that moment, I knew Leksi wanted to take me but there was fear in her eyes. She feared being punished. And I do not want to get my dear Leksi into trouble. I had no choice but to stay behind while having a grudge against the teacher and headmaster—I hope they are struck by lightning. Leksi and I have been inseparable since birth. We used to share space in the *noken,* the bag woven from wood fibers used as a sling carrier, food, and even the love of Mace and Mabel.

This morning, I said goodbye to Leksi at the end of the street, watching her figure dressed in an oversized uniform slowly disappear in the crowd of people and vehicles. That figure will return around naptime. And it will be soon. I will wait.

LEKSI

I asked Mabel and Mace why I had to go to school. They both said it would make me smart.

"You'll be good at reading, writing, and counting. That way, no bad shopkeeper can cheat you when you buy candy," said Mabel.

"Smart people can make their lives better, richer and more prosperous. Just so you know, that is everyone's ultimate dream in this world," Mace added while tightly braiding the hair on both sides of my head.

"Ouch!" I screamed a little, holding back the pain.

Mace pulled another handful of my hair that made my scalp tight and my eyes feel like popping out.

"She's right. Listen to your mace. Parents always do the best for their children. That's why you have to go to school," added Mabel, still with a sweet voice.

I still didn't believe them. With pain on my face from the braiding, I said that Mabel is good at reading and counting, and even speaking a foreign language, but she never went to school. I also told Mace that my ultimate dream was not being richer.

"I don't know what prosperous means, Mace, but I know a better life is when people throw parties and they invite us, and when you let me play all day long without having to go to school." I said the last part as my way of not wanting to go to school. Then I said, "I've never dreamed about being rich, Mace. Not even once." I shook my head.

Hearing that, Mabel and Mace asked what my dreams were.

"I often dream of playing with Pum and Kwee, and walking to the market with them. In my dream last night, I won a race over Yosi. She cried because she lost and she had to give all her candies to me." I laughed when I thought about this coming true. Yosi is an unbeatable runner. She lives next door. Being faster than her would be something to be proud of. I puffed my chest with pride as if I had really won the race while Mace finished braiding my hair.

"Give it a rest, Leksi. You have to go to school, period. No argument." Mace pushed me off her lap. She said that every *Komen* woman has to take care of the family, house, and field, and every child has to go to school. Mace returned the comb to the bedroom, and talked to herself about how she does not want me to have the life of a native Papua woman. She would be very proud if I went to high school later and wore the white and grey uniform just like the kids she sometimes meets on the road to the market.

"If that's what you really want, Mace, just buy me a grey skirt. I have the white blouse already. I'll wear them right now so you can see me and be proud. What do you say?" I followed her from the bedroom to the kitchen for breakfast and wondered if I would look pretty wearing that dull colored outfit.

No one expected to hear Mabel laugh in the living room. I jumped in surprise and so did my piggy, Kwee, who ran and hid in the bedroom.

"Oh my, Lisbeth. Your daughter is so smart, really smart," Mabel exclaimed between fits of laughter and slapping her thighs. "She's just like her father. Yes, yes, just like him. You realize that, right?" But then suddenly, as if someone had just told her to be quiet because a baby slept in the next room, her voice turned soft. "Ah, Johanis. What an insolent boy." Her voice returned to being loud when she turned to Mace. "Oh, Lisbeth. Please forgive this old Mabel for reminding you of him, dear. I'm sorry."

Like a thick fog rolling down the mountain, silence spread through the house. It turned Mabel's laughter into unclear mumbles and Mace's breathing into sighs. Trapped in the awkwardness was me. I never understand this. It happens every time someone talks about my dad or accidentally mentions his name. I imagine him like a ghost that no one should mention and something bad happens to anyone who does. Maybe my dad was a scary man, or even non-human. Ooohh… I felt goose bumps all over my body.

What made me want to go to school that morning was different from the days before. Mace did not have to threaten me with her sour face, and neither did Mabel have to sweet-talk me. I give up half of my playing time for school just to see the happiness on their faces. Mace has had a sad face ever since she heard dad's name. Without them knowing, I promised myself to never be as smart as my dad again or be anything like him. This is so there will be no need to ever say his name again and we can keep our smiles.

I did not like the man I had never seen in my life, my dad.

***

"Did you have fun at school, Leksi? Did they teach you the letter O?"

Like usual, every time I returned from school, Pum and Kwee waited for me in the yard. Mabel was inside the house getting her vegetables ready to sell at the market.

I saw Yosi behind the slightly parted curtains next door. She must have been waiting for me to ask her to play.

Every time I came home from school, Mabel always asked the same questions. So, I gave her the same answers. "It was fine, Mabel, like what you said." Then I told her what I learned that day. Since I had learned the letters K, L, M, and N the day before, Mabel guessed that I learned the letter O. Yes, she was right. I did learn that. But she is wrong about having fun and I lied about school being fine.

My school is far from home. I have to walk the dirt road of my village until I reach the busy paved asphalt street, cross over, and pass the soccer field and a few houses. Then I go through the open market that is always busy and a little muddy, until I reach a three-way junction where I turn left, walk straight, cross the bridge, and walk straight again until I get to the migrants' housing complex. I turn left again, and not far from a cassava field, there is my school. Mace took me only during the first week. I have done it by myself ever since.

Walking that far does not really bother me, especially since I wear shoes. The shoes are a little big for me, but never mind, they are a gift from one of Mabel's customers who heard I was going to school. The problem is I do not like walking alone. I want Pum and Kwee to come with me. Yosi would be okay too, but she stays at home instead of going to school. She said her parents couldn't afford the uniform. I know she lied. Some of my classmates don't wear a uniform, yet they were allowed to go to school.

Yosi's parents don't let her go to school because she is a girl. She has to take care of her three younger brothers and sisters and help her heavily pregnant mom around the house and in the field. I feel bad for her, especially since she is older than me.

Once, I told Yosi about my school. The walls are made of white-painted wooden planks, just like most of the houses in our village. The roof is made of metal sheets that turns the room into a furnace during the day and causes it to be awful noisy when it rains. A few of the sheets are loose so there are holes through which I can peek at the sky above. But when it rains, those holes cause leaks that make my classroom all wet or even flooded.

"Somebody has to cover those holes with something, Leksi, before your classroom turns into a well," Yosi told me, sounding so concerned.

I don't think it is necessary yet, because there are many more holes in my school. I can't tell Yosi before I know the exact number of the holes. I want to surprise her, just like she was surprised to learn about the picture high on the wall in our classroom of a bird that has seventeen feathers on its wings, eight on its tail, and forty-five on its neck. I told her exactly what Pak Wenas, our teacher, told us.

"Wow, that bird sounds so cool. It can fly with only seventeen feathers on each wing. But even cooler is the person who counted all those feathers. Who was that, Leksi? Was it your teacher?" After that conversation, every time she throws a stone and manages to catch a bird, she has to counts its feathers. It goes the same for chicken and ducks.

Unlike Yosi, I am more interested in the pictures on the left and right side of that bird, of two paituas wearing black hats. Pak Wenas said those fatherly looking men were the president and vice president of our country. I don't remember their names, only their hats.

Those hats made me think real hard. What if *Pace* Arare, the head of the village, wore a hat like that? I mean, everyone in the village knows Pace Arare lets his hair grow into something that resembles a blossomed cauliflower. If he became the president and had his picture taken, how would he wear the little black hat? Would he put it on top of his big frizzy hair and use bobby pins to hold it in place, or would he choose a hat made from colorful feathers that Komen men usually wear at the traditional festivities? If you asked me, I prefer him wearing the feather hat to the black hat. It suits him better, and makes him look very manly. I like manly guys. One day I will marry one, but not Pace Arare, of course. He is already old.

I also told Yosi about my crowded, always noisy, and damp classroom. Imagine sixty students in one room. I counted them. Three students, sometimes four if they are small enough, share a bench in the class. That is why, when it is time to take notes, some place their books on the desk to write, while others put their books on their knees. I am lucky to share my bench with only two other students. I sit in the middle. I can write on the desk, and that is good. What is not so good is that I have little space to move. Unless I want to listen to my bench-mates complain, I have to choose whether to put my arms on or under the table during the lesson.

Mabel should take me to school so she could see that it isn't fun, and never ask me the question again. She also needs to get into the class with me to understand that playing is more fun than studying, which is nothing but sitting for hours. I learn my letters and numbers at school, but I'm too tired to play with Pum, Kwee, and Yosi. That is what I don't like. Going to school makes me learn many new things, but I am behind in what happens in the village and the market.

Before Mace sent me to school, I spent my time playing or walking around the village, sometimes as far as the market and the big street that was forbidden to me. I went there secretly of course, because Mabel and Mace would scold and punish me if they found out. I took Kwee and Pum along since I knew they would not tell.

I did not ask Yosi because she is a big coward. She said she heard from the mamas that the big street leads to a place where the ghosts live. A kid should never go there alone, because he or she will be run over by the ghosts' cars. Those cars have tires as big as the largest river stone you have ever seen and a pair of lights as bright as the sun. But from what I know, there are only different types of cars on that street. Their tires are big but nowhere as big as a large river stone. Maybe it is different at night, because I only go there during the day.

Maybe the ghost's car that Yosi mentioned only goes out at night when everyone is asleep, or maybe she made it up so I will never leave her alone. She doesn't know I went to the big street, hoping to see my dad walk from his house on the end of the street at Mount Nemangkawi. The spirits of Amungme people return there after they die. I just wanted to see my father's face to find out if he was as scary as a ghost and that was why Mace and Mabel didn't want to speak his name.

"Your father is dead, Leksi. Don't think about him or even mention him," I still hear Mace say.

I wonder if this feeling is what they called longing.

Chapter 2

LEKSI

Although I am only seven years old, Mabel and Mace have put many expectations on my little shoulders. As a mother, Mace wishes for me to grow into a lucky and educated young woman, though I am sure she didn't have this on her wish list when I was born. She never went to school and only learned the word "educated" from the young people who came to our house on one hot day about a year ago. They were neatly dressed and smelled good.

They said hello to me, spoke politely, and smiled when they asked if my mother or father was home. I was the one who went to the door, and I looked at them without a bit of trust. They were strangers. I knew from their light skin and straight hair that one or two of them were immigrants.

Mace and Mabel had warned me about being extra careful with strangers, especially immigrants. That was why I stayed at the door and left only a small crack for me to peek through. I said coldly, "My father is not here. No one is home."

I meant what I said, but they laughed. To show them, I put on my hardest serious face. I wanted to look like the vegetable sellers at the market when they have difficult customers and say, "You cannot bargain with me, ma'am. I will never lower the price, not even when I am dead." My serious face only made one of them come closer. She bent down to my level and said with a pleasant voice that they meant no harm. They only wanted to talk to my parents. I was surprised and took a few steps back. It was a good thing that Mabel, who was getting ready to sell her vegetables, suddenly appeared. She talked on the porch with them. I peeked through the open door, a little scared but I wanted to know more.

They introduced themselves as members of a non-governmental organization downtown. One of them explained that they were there to help all the villagers have a better life.

"Our life is just fine. We don't need your help," Mabel said sternly. She was very careful. I knew she was testing them and trying to find out what they really wanted.

She told me that if a guest meant harm, how they stood and what they said would tell me. The same thing went for a guest that meant well. Even if the guest hid their bad intentions, Mabel could sense it. Although she never admitted it, I knew she could do magic. Her kind of magic gave her the power to read someone's heart or mind, just like being able to know an egg is bad without breaking it.

Mabel trusted the visitors and believed they had good intentions. When they came back on another day, she gave them a warm welcome.

"If someone promises to make you richer, slam the door in his face. But if he promises you to make you smarter and better, let him in. It's fine to refuse money because the devil might hide in it, but only a fool says no to free knowledge. Knowledge is far more important than money, child. Remember that," she said when I asked why she treated those people so nice.

Mabel and Mace became close friends with them, and took me on a Sunday to a meeting in the big hall of the head district's office. That place was far from our house but Mace and Mabel were eager to go. They wore their best outing clothes—so did I—and brought their purses. Many mamas were there, and other children like me. We sat still on our chairs because we didn't know why we were there. The meeting was not a party, a church service, or a school.

"Can you be good today, child? Listen to what they say. They will teach us new things. So pay attention," Mabel whispered when I started to move in my chair next to hers. I always get restless whenever I sit and do nothing for too long. It's like a boil suddenly appears on my butt and I want to pop it by running around or playing.

"Today we will learn about the deadly malaria disease, the causes and how to treat and prevent it."

A young woman with skin was as black as night, not that different from ours only fresher, talked in front of a wall that lit up and showed pictures. She pointed to the wall while the pictures kept changing.

I forgot about my imaginary boil for a while. My mouth fell open in surprise. In front of my eyes was the mosquito they said caused malaria, and it was gigantic. The straight antenna looked like the one for Pace Arare's radio, and it had an ugly striped bulging belly.

"No wonder you went to the hospital when you caught malaria, Mabel. It's a giant mosquito. You are lucky not to have your blood sucked dry," I whispered.

Mabel only nodded.

***

After the meeting, Mace, who was surprised and interested with what she had seen, suddenly spoke her wish. She wanted me to be like the smart young woman who explained about mosquitoes and malaria.

"You must study as much as possible, Leksi, so you can be like her." Mace looked at the woman like she was her own daughter. "Mabel and I will be so proud if you are as smart and successful as her. That is why you have to go to school and study. Everything else can wait."

A few months later, they sent me to school.

Mace's wish was very different from my friend's mothers, especially Yosi's mother. The other mothers wished their daughters would be the luckiest bride, no matter how ugly, skinny, or hunched over their daughter will be from carrying too many heavy loads on her head. According to those mothers, a daughter's fortune only comes from a wealthy and respectable man. It makes no difference if he is young and a drunkard, or is old and has many wives. Being poor makes that wish into a mantra they chant every day, believing that someday it will come true.

"You can't mend a broken fence in the field by hoping someone will do it for you. You have to fix it yourself before a boar attacks and destroys all you have," Mace said every time I told her over dinner about the latest gossip I heard from the villagers. I always did that. I told everything I saw or heard when I was out playing, buying snacks at the shop, or wandering around.

The mamas are usually busy gossiping on their porches after a good nap. In the middle of threats shouted at their kids who always hit and wrestle one another while playing, and the rhythm of cardboard or old newspapers used to fan their sweaty bodies, the mamas exchange many stories, jokes, nonsense, wishes, hopes, and even curses during noisy mid-afternoon conversations.

I learn which pace came home drunk that morning, which mace has to stay in the house because her husband beat her all night, and which house will hold the next *bakar batu* party.

"Never eavesdrop on an adult's conversation, Leksi. Not good. They may get angry and even hit you when they find out," Mace scolded me after I told her I heard Pace Yakob's son was arrested. But I don't care.

Gathering news is an exciting game. I want to find the biggest news of all time, and when I tell Mace, she will exclaim, "Oh my God. Is that true, Leksi? I'm grateful to hear this from you and not anyone else."

Mabel has her own wish for me. She really wants me to grow up as healthy and big as her. It's true. She often dreams of feeding me bread, cheese, and milk, the kind of food she used to eat.

"Those foods made me this big but now I can only afford taro, sago, sweet potato, and cassava, and meat when someone is throwing a party. I will work very hard so I can buy you bread, cheese, and milk. Be patient, child. I will make you just as big as I am." She looked at Kwee like he should know.

When Mabel is in that mood, my bedtime story is all about bread, cheese, and milk. Only rich people enjoy those foods. Mabel tells her stories and smacks her lips, like she just had them for dinner and a little taste had stayed in her mouth.

I sometimes smack my lips as I listen to her, and try to imagine what they taste like, but I can't. I know what bread and milk look like—I can't say the same about cheese—but I've never tried any of it.

Mabel told me that eating a slice of bread is like eating the softest and most tender sago cake in the world. It is also a little sweet. When cheese is added to the bread, it tastes sweet and salty. That sago cake melted right away in your mouth.

"That's impossible, Mabel. Sago is never soft," I said.

It's hard to imagine something that different from what I know. I have to change it to something that matches my imagination. It's like picturing a sun shaped like a triangle, when I know the sun was round, or imagining Komen people with skin as light as some of the immigrants, which resembles the color of a freshly plucked chicken. It's hard.

The sago I eat is hard and coarse, so I have a hard time imagining it to be soft, let alone mushy. The sweet and salty taste is too much for my imagination because sago is tasteless. I asked Mabel to change how she thought they were alike, with the kind of taste that is easy to imagine and doesn't go against what I know.

"You need to learn how to see something without using your eyes, child, and use your other senses instead, like the nose. And always use your heart and mind. Okay, I will make it easier for you. Try this," she said. "Close your eyes and think of the shape of sago."

I closed my eyes and started imagining.

"Well? Do you have the shape?"

I nodded.

Next, she asked me to picture the sago with grains so fine that they would go through a tea strainer. That pile of soft sago, she said, is turned into a cake by mixing it with a lot of sugar, a little salt, and beaten eggs. The round and thin cake is then baked on a very hot stone.

"Imagine the scent of that sweet omelet. You can, right?"

I said yes and my mouth filled with sweet saliva.

Still talking to my imagination, Mabel told me to guess what the imaginary sago cake would taste like.

I said it had to be good and I licked my dry lips.

"How do you know it is good?"

"Because I think so."

"Is it because of the scent of the sugar and egg?"

I thought for a moment. "Maybe," I said.

Mabel told me to open my eyes, and gave me her warmest smile. She said, "You just saw something with your nose, heart, and mind."

I frowned. The whole idea is too complicated for me. I tried very hard to look at my own nose. I couldn't see it, not even the tip. Maybe mine is too flat. I only wanted to make sure if my nose could really see, that is all.

She stopped me when my eyes were crossed. "That's not what I mean, child, not like that." Holding back her laughter, she said, "One day you will understand what I mean, Leksi. Looks can be deceiving. What looks good may not be good. What seems calm can still hide a current in its deepest end. What seems nice outside may be rotten inside."

"Like a worm inside a shallot?" I said.

Mabel gave me a wise nod and stroked my head with her crooked left fingers.

"You're right, child. Like a worm inside a shallot."

That night I fell asleep dreaming of cheese-flavored sago and shallots that tasted like worms.

PUM

I stand near Leksi's bed as Mabel tells her about bread, milk, and cheese. I stay there when Mabel tiptoes away after Leksi has fallen asleep and in passing pats my head. "Look after her, Pum," she said. "She's still too fragile to survive this cruel world."

I send her a reassuring look, showing that I will even without her asking. I have always considered Leksi as my own child.

Mabel smiles and walks away. I watch her big body disappear in the folds of the curtain that divided the rooms. After she is gone, I let out a sigh. We share the same worry. Her worries are mine. We are both old. Will I be able to fulfill her wish?

We have a special bond stronger than friendship or kinship. A bond forged by laughter and tears, sweat and blood, and a decade of difficult years. A bond that is stronger when we are apart and tighter when we are near. Mabel and I are like twins who shared more than the same womb; we share the same soul.

If Kwee heard me, he would say that Leksi and he also have that bond. No, no. It's too soon for him to think so. They are only kids. They have yet to see much of what the hands of fate can do, or go through life's ups and downs.

Meanwhile, Mabel and I are getting closer to the end. The finish line. We will leave everything to Kwee and Leksi. After all, the sky is not always blue, right?

Believe me when I say it never crossed Mabel's mind to be this poor in her old age. Neither did little Mabel expect to live a good life with a kind foreign family. This is true. Mabel once worked for the de Wissels, and spent her teenage life as their domestic helper and nanny. In the mornings, afternoons, and evenings when no one was home, she told me her story. Her very first journey on her own, leaving the village of her people far behind in Baliem Valley.

Mabel trusts me to be her friend and protector, as well as a reminder of the family she left behind. It's no wonder that she and I are very close. Our loyalty to each other is the envy of everyone, including Kwee.

A long time ago, I had a chat with Death when he visited me after a stray arrow had hit me in the eye. If you think Death is so frightening that he makes a fierce hunting dog like me with teeth as sharp as knives run away with his tail between his legs, you are mistaken. When I looked at him with my good eye, Death appeared sympathetic— or had my imperfection won Death's sympathy? What I know for sure is that we exchanged stories for a while. In fact, he took me for a short walk.

With Death, I saw the various paths that lead to the end of life. One path he showed me had a battlefield.

"This is how most men will end up in this era, pierced by an arrowhead, slashed by a sword, shot by a gun, or bleeding to death."

But they are heroes. They die for the honor of their tribe and people, as well as for truth and justice. That was my immediate response, but Death had a different opinion.

Then, Death took me to see another path, a killing field.

"This is how most animals will end up in this era, killed by an arrow, a bullet, a deathly trap, a sharp net, or poison."

But they are heroes too. They died to feed others, especially humans.

This time, Death seemed to want to share his thoughts. I waited with intense curiosity, but he did not say anything. Instead, he took me to the last path, the end of the road. It was a very beautiful place with amazing buildings I had never seen, scattered piles of gold as high as a mountain, a glassy smooth road connecting all the tall buildings, an orange twilight sky, and one thing I will never forget, the scent of pleasure that filled the air.

This must be the destination God has promised to those who are faithful to Him, I guessed with confidence. I secretly wished I could die in that place. It looked so extraordinarily beautiful.

But Death only responded with silence, and doubt crept in. I took his silence as a sign I was wrong. But what other truth could there have been? The path led to a wonderful end, so it could not have been for the heathen and evildoers. It was too good for them.

"This is how most living beings will end up in this era, starvation, plague, poverty, or natural disasters."

For a moment, I was speechless. I thought I had not heard him correctly. Or did he misspeak? Unfortunately, it didn't seem so.

I sensed a wrenching sadness in his words and decided to voice my doubt. *It cannot be. No human, animal, or plant dies of those things in this very beautiful place.* I threw another glance at the place to convince myself. And it was true. There was nothing strange there. *It is such a perfect place*, I mumbled.

"Yes, humans always want that. They make everything as perfect as possible, including the world they live in, for so many reasons. Unfortunately, they forget that nothing is perfect except God, the Most Perfect One. The perfection you see here is a façade. Fake. The kind of perfection that sacrifices nature. No balance, common interests, or concern for one another exists in this place. Take another look. Use your soul to see and find the truth of my words."

That was the first time I learned not to believe everything I saw, even with my own eyes. I taught that lesson to Mabel, and she had passed it down to Leksi.

Years have passed since that incident. Death did not take me to the end of my road. He said it was not my time yet. Even so, I keep in my memory the image of the last path that Death showed me, the one I considered most frightening. What is strange is that lately I feel the world moving toward that direction.

Beautiful buildings and sky-piercing iron towers sprout in the middle of our poor village. The big roads are repaired so the cars of the immigrants can pass by, yet the potholes in the road in front of our house remain untouched. Foreigners have started to mine as much gold as possible in places where we chopped sago trees open just enough for us to eat. Money is easily earned and spent. Seeing all this, I sigh more often. Are all of us, including me, destined for the pathetic end as described by Death: starvation, plague, poverty, or natural disasters where everything is constantly made to look better?

I get up and almost trip over Kwee sleeping at the end of Leksi's cot. With my good eye, I see Leksi sleeping soundly; her chest moves with the rhythm of her steady breathing. The smile on her innocent face shows that she is having a good dream. Mabel is right, the child is still too innocent and fragile to survive an increasingly rotten world.

My dear Leksi, my beloved Leksi. Sleep tight and have a wonderful dream. Today I am here to protect you. As for tomorrow and afterward, I hope to stay beside you. But if not, God will always look after you. Trust me.

I am very, very tired. I just want a good night's rest. Go back to sleep, Kwee. Don't stare at me like that. Goodnight.

Chapter 3

LEKSI

Pum is old, for sure. His fur has a patch of white, just like Mabel's hair that has almost turned all white. Those brown spots are his original fur. Pum and Mabel have been together for a very long time. People say that he was her shadow even before I was born. Wherever she went, he was always nearby. He even went with her to the hospital when she had malaria after I was born. Pum is the dog she wanted to have since childhood.

Her family had a dog when she was little. He was supposed to go hunting with her oldest brother in the forest, but the dog liked being with her. They were very close and when she had to leave her village, she cried when he stayed behind. Will Mace and Mabel let me take my pig, Kwee, if I have to leave home one day? I never think that far ahead. It's not because I'm scared. Why should I leave home if I have no idea where to go?

My house is just a simple wooden house, not that different from my school. Both are cramped and dim, and leak when it rains. But the holes in the roof of my house are not as big as the ones at my school. For any big hole, either Mabel or Mace climbs on the roof to cover it when the rains come. Since there is no grown up man in our house, we, the women, do everything ourselves.

"Why have a pace around if he only puts his man part to work and uses his hands for nothing except holding a bottle of *Tomi-tomi*, or hitting a woman? What kind of man is that? Do you want your Mace to become like Yosi's mother? She always has a swollen cheek, pregnant or not. And Yosi's legs look like a bad taro, all black and blue." That's what Mace said when I asked why she didn't remarry although some men often talk sweet to her.

"Getting married is easy, Leksi. Being married is hard," she explained.

"What is so hard about it?"

"It just is. You're too young to understand. So just forget about it."

"Just tell me, Mace. I'll understand. Come on."

Mace stopped figuring the profit from selling vegetables in the market that day. She breathed in like she was trying to have enough strength to push a big cabinet, and stared at me for a long time.

"You really want to know?"

I said yes.

"Alright, here it goes." Mace explained like a teacher in front of the class. "Getting married is easy because at first, a marriage is like a game. You and a friend agree to play the game together."

"The bride and groom game?"

"Yes, kind of. After the festivities of the wedding are over and the guests have gone home, both of you see there is a long road for you to take together. Meanwhile, the game has one rule you have to obey."

"No cheating."

"Yes, that too." Mace rubbed the top of my head. "The rule, Leksi, is you have to play the game together, all the time, every day until the end of your life."

"No holiday?"

Mace shook her head.

"Ugh, that sounds boring."

"Besides," Mace said as if she had not heard me, "both of you must also try solving any problem that comes your way. You must trust each other, be honest to each other, and respect each other. Neither one can feel they must always win or they are losing."

"But I have a friend who always wants to be first. Do you know Karel?"

"The boy who lives at the corner of the street near the candy shop?"

"Yes, that's him. Every kid in the village knows Karel because he likes to show off his toys. He also never loses any game. We often play together and he always wants to be first."

"That's not good."

"Then I don't want to get married. The rules are too difficult. I'd rather play with Yosi, especially when we pretend to be cooking."

"There you are. Just go and play outside."

From that time, I have never asked Mace to remarry.

"Being married turns out to be very hard, even harder than school. There's no holiday on Sunday or public holidays," I told Yosi in the middle of our game.

"Really? But I still want to get married. That's what I have always wanted. I'll be the most beautiful bride in the village."

"Okay, if that's what you want. But you had better not marry Karel because he never gives in and has the loudest voice. You'll go deaf if you are with him all the time."

Yosi looked at me with thanks.

"You're my best friend, Leksi. If you were a boy, I'd choose you for my husband."

"But I'm a girl."

"Okay, then we'll just be friends. Very good friends."

"Like sisters?"

"Yes, sisters. You and me."

***

Yosi is five years older than me, and we became friends as soon as I was allowed to play outside. I know more than she does because she never goes to school. If she is not at the market or in the field helping her mother, she stays at home. Her being quiet and looking at things like

34

something bad is about to happen always makes me the livelier one. Yosi is like this because of her fear of doing or saying something wrong. It does not take much for her mother, Mama Helda, to yell at her. Sometimes Mama Helda hits and pinches her. Yosi keeps quiet and takes it all, like a rock. If she died from a beating, I would probably not hear her screams. It would take Mama Helda's cry of regret to break the news.

Once I told Yosi how mad I was about how her mother treated her. I told Yosi to stand up for herself when she was yelled at for a small mistake. She often gets a beating on the leg when she is late taking the laundry in from the clothesline.

Mama Helda expects Yosi do a bunch of things at the same time. She doesn't care that Yosi has only two hands and two legs, and she has three bratty younger brothers to look after. She has to take care of them because her pregnant mother is too busy with the house and field work.

"Don't blame my mama, Leksi. She suffers too, if only you knew."

Then this story came out of her, not much louder than a whisper:

"I used to think I wasn't my mama's child, maybe a step daughter or adopted. You know why, Leksi? Because her hands hit my legs, her fingers pinched my stomach, and above all, her words hurt my feelings. It's easier to take all that, thinking I'm not her flesh and blood. I wished that one day my real mama would come and stop my hurting. My real mama would take me away. But, Leksi,

I am her real child. Old Mrs. Kewa, who helped with the delivery of my youngest brother, said that his cry sounded like mine when I was born.

"'Loud and clear, it was heard over the mountain and across the sea. When he grows up, he will make your family proud. Ask your mother if you don't believe me. I also made such prophecy for you,' Mrs. Kewa said.

"After that, Leksi, believe me or not, I hated Mama. I thought she didn't love me and that was why she treated me so bad, or she didn't want me because I was a girl. She said if her first born was a male, she would have told him to find a job being a day laborer at the market or helping out as a mason at a housing project."

She stopped like she wanted time to carry her unspoken sadness away. She sighed.

"I really want to work for money, Leksi. My family is very poor and Pace's weekly salary is not enough, even when combined with the money Mace earns selling the vegetables from our field. You know how my pace likes to drink with his friends until dawn. And Mama is pregnant again. My three little brothers are too young.

"'Are you a boy or girl? Help around the house and at the field, and take care of your brothers like other girls do. Don't think of any other nonsense.'

"That's what Mama said when I told her I wanted to find a job, any job, out there. I just want to help her and make her proud of me. I was confused and not sure of what to do. Maybe it was better for me to stay quiet. I kept my pain to myself and stayed angry with her. This was her fault. She couldn't take care of her family, so everything fell to her daughter. She also let Pace use up all the money he earned without saving any for me to go to school like other kids, like you, Leksi. If I could choose, I want God to give me a brave mama like your Mabel, or Mace, who always stands by you instead of beating you. But this changed after what I saw one night."

Yosi choked when she tried to go on. She rubbed her eyes as if suddenly dust got in them. It took quite a while to clean out that dust. Yosi's eyes were red. She blinked a couple of times, but that only brought tears. One by one, the teardrops ran down her sunken cheek and formed a white line on her dark face. She wiped the back of her hand over the tears and smiled like she was embarrassed for crying without a reason. After her smile faded, she told the rest of her story.

"The wind that night felt harsh and was also terribly cold. The chill woke me up. I poked with my feet for the thin blanket that had covered me up to my shoulders earlier. I found it and pulled it over me with my eyes still closed. I hate to open my sleepy eyes when I wake up in the middle of the night. Covered by the blanket and with my two younger brothers sleeping on each side of me, I was warm and ready to go back to sleep and my dream. But then I heard Mama's voice. She was still awake, praying. Her prayer came from the living room. You have been to my house, right? There is only a curtain between the living room and my bedroom. Well, my bedroom is actually a small room in the back that Pace turned into a bedroom. It is tiny but that's okay because we only use it for sleeping at night.

"I knew Pace was not home yet. During those days, we heard about so many people who were arrested in the middle of the night for no reason. That's why she prayed. She prayed for Pace's safety, for him to return home so our lives would go on. I prayed along with her that night, although I don't remember exactly what I said. I had not finished my prayer when a loud banging on the door disturbed the quiet night. I heard Mama scream and I jumped a little. I could hear their voices.

"'Dear, you are back?'

"'Of course I am. Can't you see me standing here? Are you blind? Huh?'

"Pace was drunk again, Leksi, three nights in a row. I knew because his body smelled of alcohol the next morning. Every time he gets his weekly wages, he spends it on alcohol. He only gives what is left to mama to keep. Usually he is drunk for one or two nights, except when there is a party or somebody takes him drinking. Maybe there was a party that night, or a friend was kind enough to take him out. One thing for sure, he hadn't had enough. He was really mad and asked for money to have more drinks.

"Maybe I would be better off not to have a pace, like you, Leksi. That night I learned that he used all the money he earned being a laborer for the whole week on what else but alcohol. Can you imagine working just so you can drink as much as you want? Meanwhile, Mama, my brothers, and me were only eating plain boiled taro and vegetables every single day. We didn't even have salt.

"I used to think Mama was bad at taking care of our money, but I was wrong. Pace did not know the value of money. For him, money was like newspaper that's easy to waste although hard to get.

"'Give me more money,' he said. 'My friends are waiting. Hurry up.'

"'Please lower your voice, dear. The children are asleep.'

"'Ah, never mind if they wake up. They can sleep tomorrow.'

"'But it's very late.'

"'So what?'

"'Our neighbors are asleep too. We're disturbing them.'

"Whap, came the sound of Pace hitting Mama.

"That was the first time I saw Pace hit Mama like a madman, Leksi. He usually hits her once or twice, but not that night. Don't say you can't believe me. I saw it with my own eyes. I'm not lying. I looked out from behind the curtain, scared and helpless.

"The dim light in the living room couldn't hide Mama's hurt face. I can still see it. Pace beat her as if he was beating a mattress left in the sun to dry. I felt terrible for her and I bit my lip to keep from crying. Her pain and helplessness went to my heart, especially when Pace threatened to hit us kids if she refused to give him money. I felt her fear.

"I waited to be his next victim when Mama gave in. I heard her drag her feet and open a tin. She gave him her savings.

"'This isn't enough,' he said. 'I want more. Why are you so stingy to your own husband?'

"'That's all the money we have, dear. No more.'

"'What did you say? No more? How come? Are you cheating on me? You better watch out.'

"I heard Mama mumble. Maybe she said no because Pace hurt her again and cursed her. Leksi, suddenly I was no longer afraid. I was mad. Yes, mad. I was so angry with the drunkard who beat my mama in the living room. I wanted to hit him with anything I could find, a pair of sandals, the mirror on the wall, the chair, or the stone we use as a doorstop.

"My anger made me blind, Leksi. My feet started to move. I held a sandal in my hand and opened the curtain. That was when Mama showed her love for me. She let him kick her as he got angry seeing I had the guts to fight him."

Yosi let her tears fall down her face. I couldn't comfort her because I didn't know what to say. Her story was scary and sad at the same time. I wanted to cry too. I thought Mabel and Mace would cry when they heard the story from me, but I was wrong.

"Mace, the story should make you cry. Why aren't you?"

"Because I'm too tired."

"What about you, Mabel? I never see you cry."

"As long as I can remember, child, I seldom cry. Crying only makes me weaker, and I do not want that. I feel bad for Mother Earth when we shower her with our tears. The water becomes salty. Plants and crops cannot grow. The animals in the forest decrease, and the sky turns cloudy. Good fortune never arrives when we cry all the time."

Maybe that is why Yosi's family is not getting ahead. Her brothers always have a reason to cry.

Chapter 4

PUM

Children nowadays grow up so fast. I'm not talking about their bodies, but how they talk, behave, and think.

I go with Leksi and Kwee to the market. Honestly, I don't really want to do this. It's my nap time. Plus, the weather is so hot, it makes the road we take seem wavy and sizzling. The same thing goes for the zinc-covered roofs. A little reflector for the sun is what they are. I am smothered in this heat. And the wind, right when I need it the most, refuses to blow. I wonder if it takes a nap. If it does, I'm jealous. My old body pines for my usual napping place on a hot day like this, the shade under the mango tree in front of the house. But my obligation to Leksi forces me to go to this wet, overcrowded, and constantly noisy place—the market. Leksi says she wants to check on Mace to see if she needs help since there are plenty of vegetables to sell today. Some rows of *petatas* are ready for harvest. However,

Mabel left the house about an hour ago to sell pinang at the busy crossroads. The way I see it, Leksi could have asked Mabel to take her to see Mace. Instead, she was just quiet. So I guess she does this on purpose. She wants to wander around.

Children.

But going with Leksi turns out to be a good thing. We met a few troublemakers on our way, a group of teenage boys forcing other kids to surrender their pocket money. The boys did this casually, even laughed, as if it was as fun as wading in the river. This saddens me. They might do the same thing to Leksi or tease her because, frankly, my Leksi is a sweet girl. The thing is, I don't have the heart to hurt them even if they hurt her. I always believe there are no bad or mean children. The circumstances change them. Their parents may not give them enough attention. The adults in general don't care, the neighborhood is simply unfriendly, or maybe all of the above.

Children are like cotton. They absorb everything around them, be it seawater or dirty water in the gutter, white or black, good or evil. I'm not surprised to know many girls, including Yosi, dream of becoming a bride, or a servant. Meanwhile, the boys want to be the number one, a champion. Ugh, what a feeble couple men and women make. Just like a man and his sandals, a wagon and its wheels, a king and his doormat. One of them loves to oppress and the other is willing to be oppressed. A champion husband and a servant wife. Hah! How chaotic this world will be if people pass this habit on from one generation to the next. The men prove their greatness through punches and swear words, and the women willingly accept this.

What is really going on?

I realize this is wrong. It hurts me to see a wife beaten up by her husband. Just so you know, no matter how fierce I was, I never harmed the mother of my children. Just ask Mabel because she knows. I loved and protected her and my kids. Isn't that the duty of a husband? To love, not to harm. To provide for her, not finish her off. You shouldn't be surprised to find most men here act that way. They hold a shared principle that love is best shown through violence. This embarrasses me. They should be more embarrassed than me, but no. They're numb.

Actually, I don't want talk about this because it's like revealing the family secrets. What else can I do? I let this out now before it's too late, hoping it will change. I know my days are numbered. Although I may still live another few years, I'm not strong enough to make a difference. Only the smart and compassionate can—and they are very few, since most are smart but don't care enough. Mabel is one of those few people. Too bad, she's old now. She used to be tough and fearless. She was never afraid to speak her mind and fight when she was right. Well, she's still like that. That's why the people in this village, both men and women, respect her. Even the fiercest paitua doesn't want to mess with her. Only after Leksi was born did she start to hold herself back.

"There comes a time when a warrior must retreat, Pum. Not to give up, but to prepare their successor. I have great hopes for Leksi. I know she has my blood, a warrior's blood."

This is why she will do any kind of job to pay for Leksi's education and her needs. Mace helps, of course. Mace works on Mabel's vegetable and petatas field from morning to noon and sells the harvest at the market until dusk. Meanwhile, after doing house chores, Mabel goes and sells the pinang she makes herself although she relies on someone else to gather the areca nuts from the tree.

"I hope Leksi isn't like most girls, Pum, who think their house is a terrible place they should leave immediately by accepting someone's hand in marriage. Married at such a young age. Yes, just like them. I bet you know who I'm referring to."

I know, Mabel, I know. All my life I have seen many girls who were just children happily playing one day, but were forced to become an adult the next day. Mama Helda was one of them.

When Yosi told Leksi she wanted to be the most beautiful bride in the village, what crossed my mind at that moment was Mama Helda during the early months of her marriage. I was in my prime condition, far from being weary like now. Meanwhile, Mabel has always been her same old self: agile, healthy, and big like a plump hen. Maybe even plumper when she had a better life. There was only the two of us; Mace and Leksi hadn't joined our home yet. Next door lived a newlywed couple, Mama

Helda and her husband. They had come to our city from their village and rented a one-bedroom house the size of a pigsty.

Mama Helda was childlike and innocent, and very pretty too, with perfect sharp nose and beautiful eyelashes. Without anyone noticing, I liked to watch her. She loved to wear a knee-length sleeveless dress, a little girl's outfit that any rookie tailor could easily make. She also liked to climb the mango tree in Mabel's front yard, and when she got one of the mangos, she ate it right away. I will never forget how skinny she was. Her breasts had not fully developed yet, in contrast to their current condition that makes any clothes she wears seem ready to burst open at the front.

Like other children her age, Mama Helda loved to play, and I was her first friend in the neighborhood. When Mabel asked how old she was, a shy shaking of her head was her reply. She said she didn't know. She only shared that she was married one month after she had her first period.

"She must be very young, Pum. My guess is she's fifteen. Hopefully God won't grant her any child in the near future or her youthful looks will vanish. She'll turn old in an instant."

Mabel's words came true. Not about not having any child soon, but how aging came with her pregnancy. She was pregnant two months later and didn't even know. I can remember vaguely what happened that day. Time and old age have worn away some of my memory.

It was high noon. The sun was glaring from the top of the highest coconut tree, grilling us no matter where we were. Mama Helda just finished her chores. She walked out of the house all sweaty, and heading toward me as I lazed in the shade under the mango tree. As she walked, she tried fanning herself with her collar, a habit she still keeps. I welcomed her with a glance and let her sit next to me. After being silent for a short while, she started to talk. She complained how the heat seemed to steam her and how she felt like a half-done sweet petatas. Then she laughed at her own words and petted my back. I looked at her again. No, it didn't disturb me. I knew she was in a good mood.

Mama Helda liked to laugh and joke a lot. But that version of her only appeared when her husband left for work at the break of the dawn. When he came home not long after dusk, she shoved her childlike cheerfulness inside her pocket. She forced herself to be a mature woman, the wife her husband wanted her to be: obedient, patient, quiet, forgiving, and the list went on as needed.

Mabel had said, "If a woman wants to please her husband all the time, she had better hide her feelings on the kitchen cupboard shelf. Unless she wants to constantly cry over how badly he treats her, and forgets that she's human too."

The men of this land are brave. They never fear fighting a battle or hunting in the jungle. They are true conquerors of nature. But what I fail to understand is that they bring that power home. They turn their own wives

48

and children into their victims. It's tragic, and that's what happened to Mama Helda.

On that particular noon, the heat-stricken yet enthusiastic Mama Helda was suddenly excited when she found yellow, ripe mangos dangling from the branches right above her head.

"Pum, I want to climb and pick a few mangos," she said.

I let her. Even if I had a voice instead of a bark and said no, she would have done it anyway. Besides, I didn't want her to call me stingy. Mabel, the owner of the mango tree, always let anyone pick the fruit. But when Mama Helda placed her foot on the lowest branch, I noticed an unusual movement. Something lit up in my head, like a warning. Quickly, I got up and ran toward her. I tried to pull her down by grabbing the hem of her dress in my teeth, before she climbed too high. I was too late; she fell with a loud thud. She was a strong and only cringed a little as a bloodstain started to form on her dress. A few hours afterward I learned about her miscarriage.

She changed after that day. Mama Helda left her childhood behind and strived to be a wife who always pleased her husband, and the mother of many children. God granted all her wishes. She delivered Yosi in less than a year and she had another child almost every year for the next seven years. She saw her husband's growing belly as a proof of her success in pleasing him. Meanwhile, her own body and her breasts also grew bigger for she was always pregnant although she had two other miscarriages.

"God loves me. You see, He took three of my children but He gave me five," she told Mabel one day.

"It's not a proof of His love, my Helda. It's a warning for you and your paitua to change and try harder for a better life. Don't just make babies and neglect them. If you keep doing so, He will take the remaining five children one by one and leave only the two of you grieving and wailing. Trust me, Helda, trust my words. Don't trust those who say that the more children you have, the bigger the fortune you'll have, unless you plan to make your children work hard to pay for your life."

That's the last conversation they had. Mama Helda didn't want to see Mabel anymore. Fortunately, she still lets Yosi play with Leksi. Oh life. Why must there be fighting? I almost forgot about Leksi.

The teenagers start to act up when we pass by.

"Whip-woo! Sister, sweet sister, would you share your candy money?"

Grrr! I immediately put on my fiercest look, which sends them running away while calling me names. This old dog still has it after all.

"You scared them, Pum," Leksi complimented me.

Kwee looks at me like I have made a joke out of myself. He is the most cynical pig I have ever met.

Oh well. All that matters is that everything is good. I managed to look after you two for one more day.

"Look where you're going, Kwee," says Leksi, "unless you want to make everyone laugh by falling into a hole."

KWEE

Pum is such a show-off. I hate this old dog. I'm sure he hates me too. He likes to appear so wise and all knowing, telling me not to do this and that as if he has done everything in the world and learned the consequences. Is every elder annoying? My mother would never be like him, if she were still alive that is. But she might have been just as bad as Pum. If she was, well then, I'm glad she's gone. Dear God, I'm sorry. I don't mean to be insolent or anything. It's just that lately I'm sick of Pum. Every look he gives me seems to imply I've done something wrong. He has this bossy attitude and acts like he wants to take the place of my father.

Only in your dreams, Pum.

That dog will never be my father. Not that I want it either. We're close, that's true, but we're not blood related.

Pum is Mabel's most loyal friend, while my mother was Mace's good friend. When Mace left her village, my mother instinctively followed her. Mother thought that Mace, who was pregnant with Leksi and carried a noken with Leksi's older brother and little me inside, were going to the field or forest like always. But Mace came here, to Dollar City. I mean, Timika. Dollar City is its nickname, the one I often hear from the immigrants and gold miners. Maybe the nickname lured Mace here as well. One thing for sure, Mace came here to look for an old woman who she hoped would be her savior. Mabel.

We walked all over the city to find her. The streets were very confusing. Instead of just one, there were many streets with forks and intersections. That's how Mother told me about their journey to find Mabel. She knew the forest and each path better than the city, the home of misleading signs and scents. There were many smoky bulls too, the name Mother gave to the fast moving vehicles that hit anyone who wasn't careful. When she told me this part, I always laughed, but after a tragedy involving the bulls, recalling this makes me weep.

Leksi is not an only child. She once had a brother. He was my friend for a short while. Mace called him Lukas, a very quiet and frail boy. He coughed so hard that he cried. He was as thin as a petatas shoot. Unlike the rest of his body, his belly was huge. He was so gaunt that his eyes seemed too big for his face and bulged all the time. Lukas and Leksi's noses looked alike, the only difference being his nose was always dripping with snot, plus some dirt when it dried.

Mace is not as caring as Mabel, but it isn't her fault that Lukas died. Yes, he died four months after Mabel and my mother arrived in Timika.

"I killed that boy, Mabel. My poor Lukas."

"It's not your fault, Lisbeth. He was seriously ill and undernourished when you brought him here."

"But I should have kept him alive. He was my son. He was supposed to be strong, like his father."

"Stop it. Don't ever mention that man's name. If he's so strong, why did he run away from his family problems and put everything on your shoulders?"

"He didn't run away, Mabel."

"Stop defending him."

"He only needs time to think."

"True, thinking about leaving you and the kids. He's just like his father, a man who can conquer the wilderness but is unable to care for his family."

"I'm sure he'll come back one day."

"He neglected you long before he left."

"One day he'll miss his children and come looking for them."

"You said he only acknowledged Lukas."

"…he did, but Lukas is gone now. Oh, what will I do? It's my fault, Mabel. I'd even take his beatings if he was with me. I don't deserve to be a mother, or Johanis' wife."

"Lisbeth, I told you not to mention that insolent boy's name again. I'll beat him up if he has the nerve to show his face, especially if he dares lay a hand on you. Although he's my son, he has deeply embarrassed me. I am ashamed to face you, Lisbeth. I really am."

This conversation happened on a gloomy evening, two days after little Lukas' funeral. Their voices escaped through the door cracks. I was still awake so I didn't have a choice but to listen in.

Hey little piglet, go to sleep, Mother squealed.

I'm not sleepy.

That's an excuse. You just want to hear what the adults are talking about, am I right?

No.

So?

I just want to know if it's true that the baby in Mace's belly isn't her husband's.

Shush. Watch your mouth, Kwee.

But I want to know, Mother.

She sighed. *That's what you get when you eavesdrop. You get the curiosity disease. When you die, I'm sure you'll be a ghost.*

Mother, you scare me. I pretended to sulk before I continued my nagging. *Come on, tell me. You must know.*

She tried to dodge my plea. *I wasn't there.*

I'm sure you know. I bet Mace told you. You're her closest friend. Tell me, Mother. Pretend it's a story that never happened.

You're such a sweet talker, she said.

Under the misty sky that evening, she promised me to tell the story when I was older.

***

"Kwee, watch out."

Who is calling me? Is that Leksi?

Out of nowhere, a big splash of dirty water comes right at me. I try to get away but can't escape completely. Part of me still gets wet. Although shocked, I catch a glimpse of a shadow moving beside me. Then I realize what has happened. A passing car splashed me with the ever-present dirty pothole water. Damn it. I'm mad, but why do I also feel like crying? Maybe it has to do with a feeling I have that is rooted in the past, one that makes it hard for me to make a sound or breathe. I freeze. I know what just happened. The image won't leave my head. Meanwhile, I tremble in fear, imagining that it could have happened another way. I only manage to take control of myself in the next second. I push my sadness aside and let out my anger. Getting angry feels a lot better than crying, because, like Mabel said, crying only makes one look weak.

"The car's gone, Kwee," says Leksi as she watches me looking right and left, trying to find the car I'd like to curse. I need to let go of this anger and the car should be at the receiving end.

"It was moving so fast. I was shocked too. Luckily, you're okay."

Leksi tries to clean me up with her tiny hands. I am touched and calm down a little. But when I hear laughter from the bystanders, my anger returns.

Pum gives me a look that says: *Let it go, Kwee. Just accept that you're dirty. If you had watched where you were going, you wouldn't be like this.* This sends me over the edge. I direct my anger at him.

Pum laughs, as much as an old dog can laugh.

He moves along, leaving Leksi who tries to coax me to keep walking.

"The market is nearby, Kwee. It's not that far. You can see it from here."

This is the first time I hate going for a walk. I want to go home.

Home. A safe place.

Chapter 5

LEKSI

I walked to the market again, but this time with Mabel and Pum. Kwee refused when I asked him to come along. He wanted to stay and guard the house. He is probably afraid of having another accident like yesterday. I think he's still scared. Kwee never worries about getting wet and dirty, but that car almost hit him. It was so close. If I hadn't yelled, and if he hadn't walked toward me, he would have ended up like his mother who died after being run over by a car a few years ago. Poor Kwee. Since then, he hates cars.

"He needs to be more careful when he's out in the street."

That's what Mabel said when I told her about yesterday. She said that while looking at Kwee sit quietly in the corner and stare at the wall with a sad face.

"Kwee is sad, Mabel."

"How do you know?"

"From his face."

"He always looks like that."

"Really?"

"It only changes when you give him food."

I laughed. Mabel tried to make light of things but Kwee refused to move. We locked the door from the outside and he became one with the house.

Mabel and Mace harvested lots of vegetables this week. They picked rica and some greens. Mabel's vegetables are big, just like her. Big and glossy, like the spring onions, tomatoes, and rica I arrange on the small table at the front of our stall. I like doing this. I group them based on their color. The ones with bright colors go in front, and the other ones go behind. I pile the green ones in the basket and arrange the rica and tomatoes by the handful because people usually buy only one or two handfuls. I don't think they like their food spicy. But spicy food tastes so good. It makes you want to eat more.

"*Rica* is expensive these days. Customers only buy as needed," Mace says as she fixes the loose bundles of *kangkung*. A customer had untied these earlier, and picked out the branches with fresh leaves and fat stems. "That's what the worms like. I can't stop the worm from visiting the kangkung. I can't stay the whole day in the field to keep it safe from worms. The worms and I, we both have our things to do."

Mabel comes out of the next-door stall and says to Mace, "We don't need to worry anymore. That company has made a deal with our people. They said they want to buy our vegetables for their workers. We actually made big money from the last harvest. They bought everything. That's how we can send Leksi to school and fix the wall of our well."

Mabel lets out a proud sigh. She pauses a little, her face shining with pride and joy as she enjoys the moment. I watch her flared nostrils that move like a fish's mouth. Luckily, there are no mosquitoes or flies around. I'm afraid those bugs will get sucked in and get trapped inside her dark nostrils. She would be tickled when they tried to escape. My nose starts to feel itchy, so I scratch and pick it as well.

"Just wait and see," Mabel says. "Soon someone from the company will come and take the vegetables. That's why I prepared the ones they're going to take."

As she massages her crooked left fingers, Mabel looks at the bamboo baskets filled with vegetables lined up near her sandals. Mabel prefers to walk barefoot just like me, except Mace gets angry with me when I do. "And then, Leksi," Mabel says to me, "after we sell all the vegetables, I'll cook you a chicken. You said you wanted to have chicken, like the kind you saw those people eat in the food stand over there. I remember what you said, child."

I look at Mace as if she caught me doing something wrong. She gives me a certain glance I don't understand. Is she mad? She often tells me not to stare at people while they are eating.

"A whole chicken is so expensive. One hundred thousand rupiah for one whole *ayam kampung*," Mace mumbles to herself while she tidies the vegetables.

"My goodness, that much?"

"Has been for a long time. Plus, the prices for everything have increased."

Then they talk about eggs.

I finish arranging the vegetables and have no idea what else I should do. I reach for the rica resting on top of one another and pull the stems from the pods, and throw them as far as possible. Deep down, I worry about eating chicken because it costs too much.

"The price of eggs went up too. It's fifty rupiah for a tray now; used to be around twenty."

"One tray? Thirty eggs?"

"Yes, thirty. Leksi, stop ruining the rica."

She surprises me. Mace has a pair of eyes in the back of her head. She couldn't see me because she is bent over, arranging the neatly tied kangkung inside the basket. I let go of the rica in my hand and decide to play under the table. Maybe I'll find something interesting.

"So how much is one egg?"

"Figure it out, Mabel. I don't know such things. Or ask Leksi. She goes to school."

"Oh right. Leksi."

Mabel's voice is like thunder. A few customers hear her and turn their heads, thinking she's calling to someone far away behind the mountain. How powerful her voice would be if that were true. I stick my head out from under the table while chewing pinang. Because my mouth is too full to speak, I look at her with wide eyes to ask what she wants me for.

"What are you doing there, huh?"

"She found your hidden pinang."

"Oh, what a little safecracker," Mabel says with understanding. I give her a wide red grin. Eating pinang dipped in limestone powder takes my mind off the possible end to my chicken-eating plan.

"Can I finish your pinang, Mabel?"

"Oh sure, child. Chew all you want. Soon we'll have money from the vegetables, and it won't be just pinang you can eat all you want. Eggs too, or maybe chicken if I can bargain a little. Ah, yes, chicken. I haven't had any for a long time. I don't even remember the taste. Ah, chicken."

***

Nobody likes waiting, not even ants and I'm sure about it. Just look at them. They would rather say, "Excuse me, coming through," and shake hands with their friends moving toward them, than wait at one spot until there are no more ants coming. I don't like waiting either, not for the vegetables to sell or for the company guy Mabel said would buy everything. My feet grow itchy from sitting on this wooden stool near our stall. I want to take a walk. Anything is better than waiting with flies buzzing around and mosquitoes trying to suck my blood. But how can I escape when Mabel and Mace are looking?

A fussy customer of Mace's comes to the stall, and she takes care of what they ask for in just one breath, getting this and grabbing that. She ignores the next customer on purpose. "The customer is king, and the loyal customer is god. Let other things wait for a moment," is how she explains what "customer" means.

Mabel is busy fanning herself with a piece of cardboard and quickly wipes off the sweat on the back of her neck. She moves to the next customer with a smile.

"What can I get you, child?" She sounds so sweet.

This is the perfect time to escape. I move away from Mabel and her customer as they bargain about the right price for a large number of tomatoes.

"How many are we talking about?"

When she says that, I'm already far from the stall. Thanks to Mabel's loud voice, I still hear her although the noise of the market starts to drown it.

Without looking back, I squeeze my way between the sticky, sweaty market people and their clothes damp with sweat stains at the back, neck, and armpits. I pass a butcher who enjoys a cigarette while cutting a big chunk of fresh meat with his large knife, a customer who candles an egg and the nagging egg seller who gets offended, and also a bald-patched stray cat about to steal a fish. I walk by a trendy but terribly smelly mama, and a limping young man with a miserable look who tries to make his way through the crowd while his hand is busy feeling the pockets and wallets of the people around him. A nicely dressed madam carefully chooses her steps on the wet ground, a runny-nosed kid cries over his fallen cake, and all the vegetables the sellers left on plastics by the road are still there.

After I ignore tempting offers from food sellers, away from a group of hair accessories and colorful flip-flops that stopped me for a while, and walk past a group of thugs quarreling with a guy wearing a helmet, I arrive at a more open space. No more orange and blue plastics hang over my head. Only a faint smell of sweat, blood, and rotten vegetables is in the air. I reach the busy street by the market. Vehicles are everywhere. Some run in the street, and some are parked carelessly. My feet keep pounding the hot asphalt farther and farther. I forget that it's only me this time, no Pum and Kwee.

I reach a shopping complex and a kind young man leaving a store suddenly greets me.

"Hello, little sister. Where are you going in this hot weather?"

His skin is dark like my people but he acts like an immigrant. He wears bright colored shorts, tee shirt, hat, and a pair of huge and very dirty black boots. Next to a necklace with a swine tooth medallion on his neck hangs a faded purple little noken.

Something valuable must be inside, since it makes him walk with a puffed chest. Yosi's brother acts the same way when he wears his favorite Superman tee shirt. Every time someone passes by, he puffs his chest to show the Superman picture. But this man's tee shirt has no picture, or maybe he has lower back pain. Mabel walks that way whenever her lower back hurts. I am curious, so I stop and look at his noken. He understands my curiosity right away.

"I have the latest cellphone right here, little sister. It's the most expensive and stylish, with a radio, music, and a map. You can make a call while watching a TV show on it. Nothing can beat this. I bet even the Regent doesn't have one."

He talks like the medicine man at the market, on and on, and so enthusiastic that spit comes out of his mouth. As he speaks, his hand rubs the noken lovingly as if a precious pig were inside.

"Do you want to have your picture taken, little sister? This phone can do that too," he offers with a big and charming smile. I'm more confused than tempted.

"Why so quiet, little sister? Can't you talk? Or don't you know what a cellphone is?"

That's exactly what confuses me. His smile fades a little.

"Never seen one?"

I say no. This time, his smile turns into pity.

He carefully reaches into his noken like he's about to catch an eel in a bucket and brings out a small, black, shiny, and rectangular box. It's too good for the ugly knitted bag.

"This is a cellphone, little sister."

He holds the thing so close to my nose that I know it has the smell of new clothes. I can see the reflection of my surprise on its smooth surface.

"It can make sounds." He does something and a sound comes out.

"It can sing." This time I hear a voice singing.

"It can take a picture too."

He holds it in front of my face and I give him a frown. What is this? I hear a strange sound I can't describe and he says that my picture is ready.

"You didn't smile, so it's not a good photo." He laughs as he shows me a picture of a face that looks like me, but with a deep frown and a cone-shape mouth. It's me. The black thing he has is amazing.

"Can I have the photo?"

"Oh you can talk, little sister. You should have spoken earlier."

I smile at his joke. He's quite funny. My smile doesn't last because he won't give me the photo. He says he can only do that if he gives me the phone too. Of course I'm disappointed. I want to show the photo to Mabel and Mace. I leave him without saying another word, and walk toward the place I have wanted to visit.

The main street.

***

Karel often brags that he's been to the end of the main street.

"There's the beautiful Heaven City. No one eats pinang and the ground is clear of red spit marks. The yards of the houses are as green as the soccer fields on TV. All the children have nice toys. You have to be in a car with a certain sticker to get in. They won't let you in if you're on foot. When I visited, I was inside a big white car."

"Be careful, Karel. It's the ghosts' car," Yosi said in fear.

"What do you know? Just shut up."

Karel said he went with his dad and his dad's friend from the office, an immigrant.

"He took us to see this huge shield." He opened his arms as wide as he could. I imagined the size of the shield.

"That's it, the ghosts' war shield," Yosi said in fear once again. Karel glared at her.

"Karel," I asked for his attention, "Mabel said Holy Mountain is at the end of the main street, not Heaven City."

I told him what I heard from Mabel. The mountain is where the spirits of the Amungme people return, and I believe my long dead father is staying there too. He was an Amungme. That's why I go to the main street and wait for my father to pass by.

Karel laughed at me. "That mountain belongs to a gold company, Leksi. There are no spirits of the dead, only huge, noisy machines digging holes. That's what my father says. Maybe Mabel thinks the machines are the spirits. And you," he poked at my head, "are stupid enough to believe the story of an old woman like Mabel who never reads the newspaper or watches television."

I told Mabel everything Karel said. I didn't expect her to get mad, but she did. She was really mad. Her nagging started from the time the sun was still behind the pinang tree until the moon was high in the sky. She cursed Pace Gerson, Karel's father, calling him an ass-licker and a

Komen man who forgot where he came from. Poverty had run over his morality.

"That's what a weak person is, Leksi. Money can buy everything about him. Not just his body, but his soul. That ass-licker only shares our curly hair and dark skin, but inside, he's no longer one of us. What native of this land would be willing to give up our mountain to strangers? None. The mountain is not sago. It's not the red fruit. It's not for sale. Our land is sacred, child. Taboo. God Almighty created it just for us. You know why? Because He knows He can count on us to guard it.

"Let me tell you, Leksi, that's why our ancestors lived a simple life. They only took what they needed from nature and gave back what was left, for nature to keep and give to their children and grandchildren. To you and your future kids. It's too bad, child, among the descendants of our ancestors, we have those who surrender that treasure to strangers. Not only that, they even become one of them."

Mabel's ranting stopped when it was time for bed. Before she closed her eyes, she let out one more annoyed grumble, "It doesn't matter that we can only afford taro, petatas, and sago. We're still better than that rice-and-bread-eating Gerson who forgets that his hair is curly and his skin is dark. A person like that has a bad nature."

Only her snore was heard afterward.

***

"Where have you been, Leksi?"

"I went for a walk."

"Where?"

"The street by the market."

"Did you go as far as the main street?"

I'm trapped by Mace's question. If I say no, what if she already knows the true answer and is testing my honesty? If I say yes, I'm sure she'll get mad at me. It's just a matter of time, whether I get yelled at now or later. I bravely choose the first option while praying that a customer will suddenly come and interrupt her.

"A young man took my picture, Mace." I try to win her heart after she rants at me without anyone interrupting. The customer I pray for never shows up. While Mace scolds me, I can only look at my sunburned toes and think what color of nail polish will go well on me. Dark red or pink? Actually, I try to hold back my sadness. I can't start crying or Mace's tirade will go longer and involve other things.

"Young man? Didn't I tell you to be careful with strangers?"

"He had hair and skin the same as us. Only his clothes were like those of the immigrants, and he had huge shoes like the ones worn by the men from the company. He had a small thing inside his noken, something he used to make a call."

"Cellphone?"

"Mace, how do you know it's called a cellphone?"

"From Pak Yadi, the butcher. He has one too. His loyal customers always call his cellphone to order meat."

"Wow, that's awesome. You should also have one, and Mabel too. Where's Mabel, Mace?"

"Out. She has something to do."

"With Pum?"

"Yes, with Pum."

"What is she doing?"

"You can ask her yourself later. Now tell me more about the young man with the cellphone."

Mace doesn't want to tell me where Mabel went, and it's okay. Mabel will tell me anyway. She likely went to her friend's stall to hear some story or buy a big bag of pinang. Thinking about pinang, I suddenly remembered.

"Mace, did the man from the company who was supposed to pick up the vegetables come?"

"Why do you ask?" Mace stops paying attention to the people walking by and looks at me, surprised.

"Nothing. Just want to know."

Mace sighs.

She's very tired today. Poor Mace. After harvesting the field a couple of days ago, now she has to wait for her vegetables to sell. I decide to continue my story about the young man in front of the shop. Hopefully, it will cheer her up a bit. I say, "I didn't know it's called a cellphone. It sure is different from the public phone with the big handle and long cord."

"Of course, Leksi. If it's big and has a cord, how would it fit into a noken?"

Mace is trying to be funny, and like always, she fails. I laugh anyway to make her happy.

"His cellphone was very nice, Mace. He said it's expensive and even the regent doesn't have one. He took my picture with it, but it wasn't a good one. I didn't smile."

She holds out her hand. "Where's the picture?"

I tell her it's saved in his cellphone. If I wanted the photo, I had to take his phone too, that's what he said.

At the end of my story, Mabel guesses the young man I met could be a *Meno*.

"They come from the mountain, Leksi, and leave planting and hunting to find gold in the river where the company throws its waste. If they're lucky, they can make a lot of money. Some people say it's as much as tens of millions. They become the new rich people and buy expensive cellphones, other unnecessary things, and have fun. When money is easily earned, it's easily spent too."

Mace says the Menos usually spend their money on going to the place where the devil spends his money.

"Where is that, Mace?"

"Out there. In a room where the lights are always low and it's always foggy. In the middle of deafening spirit-calling music and the loud laughter of female devils."

"Is it at the end of the main street?"

My question makes Mace look me in the eye, as if she is trying to make sure of something.

"You're right, Leksi. At the end of that main street, everything bad gathers. Will you promise me to stop sneaking out to go there?"

This time, it's me looking Mace right in the eye. Deep down, I save a question for Mabel.

Chapter 6

PUM

Many people talk like they are passing gas. Their mindless jabbering creates a stink. I'm sure those people have filthy minds. The smellier it gets when they talk, the dirtier their minds. I don't mean their breath, of course. I'm talking about the bad odor that rises from every sentence filled with nonsense, empty promises, and slander. The effect of this kind of talk reaches deep into the heart of those who hear it and causes bad feelings.

What's strange is there are more of these people. They are getting smarter at covering up their smelly talk. It's hard to detect, even when you listen carefully, think about the truth to their words before believing them, or even ask for a series of proof. They still succeed. It's a pain, and not surprising that besides causing bad feelings, their words also shed blood.

Some of the villagers whisper behind Mabel's back that she is no longer brave, that her courage wanes as she gets older. That's not true. Her courage will not fade away like a pair of cheap dyed jeans sold at the fair, jeans that fade in the first wash. I understand her so well because Mabel tells me everything about her life, down to its tiniest detail. This is part of the bond we have, Mabel and me. An old woman talks to her old dog about her past and no one notices. I know from her stories she was born with a courage that has become stronger with time. Life has never been easy for her.

***

(Baliem Valley, 1946) The Baliem Valley was as pure as when first created. The forest remained thick, full of food and water, and as green as a new leaf untouched by worms and bugs. Its soil hid many wonders, which later tarnished the land and its people. A number of brown rivers cut through the valley, bending and twisting to the south where they emptied into the Arafuru Sea. Damp swamps that were home to crocodiles and leeches surrounded the valley. A few mountains stood as guards, proud and tall. Everyone heard nature breathe and sing. During this time, on a plain in the middle of the valley, Mabel was born and raised as one of the children of the Dani people. They called her Waya.

She was the third of four children. Her two older brothers were brave hunters. Mabel spent more time with them than her quiet and frail younger sister. Her big, tall father had muscular arms that looked like they could bend a river. His penetrating gaze, weathered face, and long sideburns only added to his stature. Those sideburns seemed to merge with the black curly hair that grew on his chest all the way to his stomach, stopping right above his *koteka*. He also had a big wide nose.

His daughter took after her father. She was proud of the man who was well known for his skill with a stone axe. Once, her father faced an extremely angry big boar. As the boar ran toward him with its horns ready to strike, he swung his stone axe at its head. The animal fell to the ground dead.

Mabel's mother was small compared to her husband although her skin was just as dark. She also had friendlier face and gaze, two things she passed down to Mabel. She wore a *sally* like most Dani women, wrapped around her big malnourished belly.

Her father kept his chest covered in shell necklaces, but her mother had nothing to show but a pair of saggy breasts that provided warmth and food for her children. She was always ready to carry anything in the worn noken that hung from her short, curly-haired head: the harvest from the field, a piglet, sago, or anything the men didn't want to carry. This habit had continued from their ancestor's time.

Only the men carried weapons because their job was to hunt and protect. Women were considered weak, so they needed protection from any enemy, but not from abuse by their own family.

Mabel grew into a tall woman built like a man, but had a sweet smile and an authentic warm gaze. She could carry many things on her head while climbing up and down the mountain bare footed, and use deadly weapons such as the spear and bow and arrow. Everyone knew Mabel was different.

Unlike most Dani children, she was like a hunting dog that hides a fierce bite behind its obedience. She might behave like a girl all day, yet at any moment Mabel was ready to fiercely attack anyone who did her wrong.

Her father asked a shaman to cast out the demon he thought was inside his daughter. The week before, Mabel had hit the chief's son in the back until he passed out. She argued that he deserved it for almost drowning her sister by holding her head under water when they were playing in the river. Mabel was still found guilty and punished. She earned a new nickname: Little Rebel.

Poor young Mabel lived in fear of what the adult women had told her, that she would never get married if she didn't change her wild behavior. She had no choice but to give in to the customs of her people.

Then came the day Mabel and her people never forgot. A group of young men ran from the forest for their lives. They showed fear worse than the fear for their meanest enemy, the *pengayau* people. As the men caught their breath, one said he saw ghosts while hunting. The ghosts looked like humans without blood. Their skin was that light and transparent.

"They're coming here," another man shouted.

The women screamed in panic like a reverberating echo. They looked to the sky and asked the Great Maker if the ghosts were a sign for doomsday or just a warning to stop neglecting Him. The only answer they heard was the crying children in their arms and squealing piglets. Dogs barked and howled. Meanwhile, the young men couldn't hide the fear on their faces. Everyone rushed home.

They put their valuables, including piglets, inside one noken and hung them from their heads as they rushed up the mountain. It was the safest place since it was close to the Great Maker.

Holding a main weapon tightly in one hand, many questions crossed the men's minds. One question was which worldly pleasure they should enjoy before the coming of doomsday? Should they eat pork until they couldn't eat anymore and have sex with their wives, or switch the order?

The ghosts had pale light skin and yellow hair, immigrants from the faraway Netherlands they learned later.

Three days after the village had run away, they returned when the sky did not fall on them. A small group of immigrants arrived at the same time.

They brought many things that caught Mabel's attention. She welcomed them with her eyes as she peered over the grown-ups who gathered in front of the men's house. Throughout the day, Mabel's mind wandered to the foreign places behind the mountains she had hoped to see as an adult, places that produced the shiny things like those the pale immigrants brought with them. Mabel was amazed at a box that produced sounds without anyone hiding inside. She didn't need to wait until she was an adult and leave her childhood to have her wish come true.

***

Piet Van de Wissel and his wife, Hermione, were a friendly Dutch couple. Mr. de Wissel introduced himself as the leader of the group. Mabel had never seen her father so welcoming toward strangers. From his words and facial expression, she knew he had fallen in love with their kindness, especially after his many gifts. Two favorites were sand-like white grains that kept everyone coming back for more (Mabel later learned it was called salt), and something that had scared everyone with its smoke because they thought it a deadly poison.

"Cigarettes. Only for the brave men," Mr. de Wissel tempted as he gave one to the chief and to a few other muscular men, including Mabel's father.

Mr. de Wissel, his wife, and his group slept and ate in a living space with a shiny roof that glowed in the dark. During evenings when the wind blew very hard, the roof made a coughing sound. Once Mable saw it fly, but not too high. Even with the strangers living far from the village, Mabel went to visit them often.

She liked to see and touch things she didn't know, things that were smooth, cold, colorful, strangely shaped, or had unique functions. For example, when they turned a set of bicycle pedals attached to a belt that turned a smaller wheel, the glass ball hanging loosely from the ceiling lit up like the sun. But more than that, she was happy to make new friends. The blue-eyed people loved her liveliness and courage, and never told her to shut up and act sweet like the adult women often told her as they gathered in front of the women's house. The sour-smelling new people never got tired of smiling and touching her head every time she did something for them, even though she didn't understand a word they said. As Mabel slowly started to understand a few foreign words, they also learned the words her people used.

During the first month after Mr. de Wissel's group arrived, many activities started in the village. Men chopped down trees with their axes, women carried rocks inside their nokens, and children played on top a big pile of sand. They were building something. Mabel overheard a conversation one evening from behind the thick bushes near the wall of the round men's house.

"This is, of course, for everyone's sake," Mr. de Wissel explained during the meeting with the chief and other men, including Mabel's father. They were constructing a "government post" and "small airport," the new words Mr. de Wissel used. "All this will bring you good, and become a heritage for your children and grandchildren to be proud of."

Mr. de Wissel explained the meaning of "government post" and "small airport" in one long, complicated sentence to the confused villagers. A dark-skinned young man, a member of his group, tried to translate twice before the oldest Dani man, who spoke many local languages, told the men what it meant in their language. Once they understood, the men buzzed with excitement and joy. Everyone wanted good things, and any man would be honored to leave something wonderful for his children.

After that night, Mr. de Wissel had all the support and help he wanted. No one stopped him. Baliem Valley stood at the threshold of change.

***

Mr. de Wissel's authority and kindness made Mabel's father and mother feel lucky when his wife, Mrs. Hermione, asked for Mabel to be their foster daughter. She would live with them and have good clothes, food, and education. Mrs. Hermione promised to never neglect Mabel, and treat her well even though her skin color was different. She said, "In God's eyes, we are all the same, brothers and sisters, a family. We need to love one another as human beings."

Mabel's mother wept as she heard the beautiful words coming from the pretty, golden-haired Mrs. Hermione, who stood in front of her. She never thought anyone would love somebody outside his or her own tribe. Since she was a child, Mabel's mother was taught about cruel tribal wars, intense hostility, never-ending fear, and belief in taboos. The new words of love rooted deeply in Mabel's young heart. Without knowing why, she believed in the miracle of love.

At the end of Mr. de Wissel's service term, Mabel followed her light-skinned family. She left Baliem Valley and her happy parents who enjoyed Mr. de Wissel's "compensation package," a number of *ots*, rolls of tobacco, bag of salt, knife, and a small thing that reflected the sunlight, a present from Mrs. Hermione to Mabel's mother. The young girl started her journey to a home behind the mountains. The place she had called home always moved from one place to another when she least expected.

The most important thing to know is that at the age of eight, Mabel freed herself from the fate of a Dani woman that only lived only for her family, husband, field, and pig.

***

(Mindiptana, 1956) Her home was in Mindiptana, an area more crowded than the valley. Mabel didn't really like it there. She lived in the *gaba-gaba* hut—a wooden shack with walls and roof made of sago leaves; the modern ones used zinc sheets for the roof, but had no ceiling. The hut was different from the stuffy houses of the men and women, where smoke and body odor filled the air. Every room had one or two big rectangular air holes she could easily climb. Still, Mabel missed her house back in the valley, except for sleeping on its damp straw floor.

She was amazed by her new surroundings, and completely in awe of the boat that took her across the river. It moved without anyone paddling. She jumped in fear when a few women came to the house wearing long white robes that seemed to float when they walked. The fragrance of soap made her spend hours in the shower or doing the laundry and dishes. She was delighted by her new name, Annabel, given to her by Mrs. Hermione because Waya, her old name, was hard for the Dutch tongue pronounce.

After two weeks in Mindiptana, Mabel showed signs of homesickness: sitting quietly in front of the house and staring blankly ahead, letting her mind wander back home to her valley.

Mabel looked much better after Mrs. Hermione scrubbed her whole body hard with soap and a towel on the first day in Mindiptana. Mrs. Hermione paid no attention to Mabel's screaming with fear and pain.

All over Mindiptana were people that looked like Mabel, with skin as dark as the night and hair as thick as the bushes, but talked in a different language. Mabel preferred to stay at home and accompany Mrs. Hermione, whose belly kept growing bigger and bigger. "We are expecting our first child," Mr. de Wissel told Mabel with a big smile on his face.

She had to learn to clean, cook, use the kitchen tools, use canned food, make a cup of hot coffee with the right amount of sugar for Mr. de Wissel every morning, and speak a little Dutch and Indonesian. Although the chores kept her busy, Mabel made time for gardening.

Mabel asked Mrs. Hermione's permission to use a small part of the backyard to plant a vegetable garden and some fruit trees. The golden-haired lady told her to use the whole backyard and Mr. de Wissel gave her a few bags of *chayote* seed he bought from who knows who. Mabel gradually forgot her home and valley. She began to feel content, but not for long.

Terrible news disturbed her peace: a massive headhunting attack had happened in a nearby village. Mr. de Wissel left the house at dawn with a few armed men without asking for his coffee or combing his hair. He forgot to change into his brown uniform until Mrs. Hermione reminded him. Mabel felt the tension rise in the air, just like when two villages were about to go to war. But strangely, she was unafraid.

Mrs. Hermione cried when her husband went away. She feared the pengayau would kill and eat him like the other victims, and skin and smoke his head before mounting it on the wall of their home.

Being in an area full of strangers, Mabel knew better than depending on anyone for help. Everyone was locked indoors to avoid a horrible death.

She collected the kitchen knives and machetes near her, and gave the lightest and sharpest knife to Mrs. Hermione, who became more hysterical. Mabel barricaded the back door with chairs and sacks of rice, sugar, and salt from the storage room.

Protecting Mrs. Hermione and her unborn child was her goal. Mr. de Wissel and she had been good to her and her parents. If the pengayau asked for a life, she would offer hers to spare Mrs. Hermione and the child.

Mabel watched over the house for next three days and nights. At dawn of the fourth day, Mr. de Wissel returned. He looked disheveled but had a smile on his face. The men caught a few pengayau and burned down their village.

The next day, Mrs. Hermione took Mabel to the trial at the court. In that crowd, Mabel saw the pengayau for the very first time. She thought she would shudder in fear, but didn't.

Maybe their tribe doesn't have any pig to eat, she thought, and that's why they eat people. She felt bad for them. Mr. de Wissel should give them pigs to raise and eat, instead of punishment.

The incident was the first sign of her great compassion.

***

(Manokwari, 1958) The de Wissels and Mabel moved again. Being a country girl, Mabel gave into her amazement. She shouted gleefully when she found out they planned to ride in a magical, giant iron bird that took people inside its stomach. When the bird flew, she screamed to get back down. The ground beneath her and the clouds right outside the window scared her.

Fortunately, her fear dissipated when she set foot in Manokwari, a village more crowded than Mindiptana.

Manokwari had many people, from black to brown, white, and yellow skinned, from those who held walking sticks and umbrellas to those who carried loads on their backs. As she watched them, Mabel realized they were fully clothed. She saw no kotekas, naked buttocks, or hanging breasts. She missed something familiar, and being there made her feel far away from home. The strangely shaped and colored buildings along the streets made it hard for her to believe she was on the same land, her sacred land. Turtles with smoke coming out of their tails moved up and down the streets to grab Mabel's attention. She later learned they were Volkswagen cars. Mr. de Wissel also had a car like that. In the front, it had two flags proudly blowing in the wind, one being orange, and the other red, white, and blue.

In Manokwari, life was better for Mr. de Wissel. His family no longer lived in a gaba-gaba hut, but in a cool building made of stone with confusing furniture, especially for Mabel. One was a box at her height that let out cold air when opened. She whispered nervously to Mr. de Wissel that he should throw away the cursed box because a ghost lived in it, and he and Mrs. Hermione hadn't seem to notice yet. Only a ghost made a person suddenly feel cold and have goose bumps all over.

Before Mabel could find a way to get rid of the box, Mrs. Hermione explained each new tool in the house. That box turned out to be a refrigerator, a machine that kept food, beverages, vegetables, and fruit from spoiling.

"In that case, Mrs. Hermione, can I put my sago in there so it will last longer?" Mabel asked after Mrs. Hermione had finished explaining. Her leaf-wrapped sago stayed inside her noken in the bedroom, not in the refrigerator.

Like I said, Mr. de Wissel's way of life had improved. One indication was the arrival of one of those smoky turtles, the Volkswagen. They often took Ann, their two-year-old firstborn, for a ride around the city. Sometimes they let Mabel join them.

Whenever that happened, Mabel wore colorful ribbons on her hair. She loved to see the different stores along the way.

Mrs. Hermione would ask her husband to stop by the bakery, butcher shop, florist, grocer, and fabric shop. Near the end of the year, the stores glistened with decorations of small lights and glossy green, red, and gold fancy paper. Mrs. Hermione and Ann tirelessly went inside each store.

Mabel followed them around with her hands full of the things they bought. Mrs. Hermione cheerfully greeted everyone she met with "Merry Christmas" and they replied with the same sentiment.

White and brown-skinned immigrants were more cheerful and friendlier during that time. They smiled and continued shopping even when a terrible thing happened in front of them.

Mabel had stepped outside the shoe store with Mrs. Hermione and Ann when they noticed a crowd gathered under the tall pinang tree. A Komen woman sat high up in the tree and wanted to end her life out of shame. The man who had promised to marry her daughter decided to break his promise. His sister had married the woman's son earlier without a dowry, but the man had too much pride to do the same. In the middle of this, some white immigrants, including Mrs. Hermione, tried to talk the woman out of jumping. They said everyone should forget their troubles on the joyful Christmas day.

"Christmas is the time for sharing our love," shouted Mrs. Hermione, using her hands as a funnel to deliver her message to the woman. "You should talk your problem through with your family."

The woman, blinded by shame, answered with a loud scream before jumping from the top of the tree. She fell straight to the ground in front of the butcher shop. Her wrecked body jerked for a moment before she died, with her head split open and her eyes bulging.

The crowd thinned out; people left one by one to continue shopping. The woman's blood, red as the lights and wrapping paper in the stores, seemed like another ornament for the joyful holiday season.

Mrs. Hermione held Ann's face close to her chest during the incident. "Forget what you saw, Annabel, or you'll have nightmares." They walked to the florist. She needed fresh flowers to decorate her house for Christmas.

"But, Madam, how could I? The woman was really…"

"Don't use Dutch. Ann is listening," Mrs. Hermione warned.

Mabel switched to Bahasa Indonesia and poured her heart out. She spoke about the heavy burden the woman carried that had made her end her life. Her body should not have been left on the street. The people should have moved it to be safe from stray dogs.

"Madam, were the people angry because she jumped when they tried to stop her? If they really want to help, now is the time. She needs them more now that she's dead, to bring her body to her family or tell them the sad news."

"The police take care of that, Annabel. Soon they will come and move the body. Don't worry about her. Now let's get going before the florist closes."

Then Mabel let it out to herself. "Did I see anyone in the crowd crying? No, right? They didn't care, or think it was their business. I saw that. Is it because she was black and they are white? Does it mean that the white God whose picture Mr. de Wissel placed in the living room wouldn't help me when I'm in trouble? I'm black. He's white."

Mabel couldn't feel the joy of Christmas that year. The holiday meant nothing more than the gift Mrs. Hermione got her from the fabric store, a new green and red ribbon to wear in her ginger, curly hair.

"Merry Christmas, Annabel."

"Thank you, Madam."

"No, no, you should say, 'Merry Christmas' too."

"Merry Christmas too, Madam."

"And to you too, Annabel."

***

(Wamena, 1960) The De Wissels moved again, this time to Wamena. Mabel couldn't hide her excitement when she found out that the place was near the Baliem Valley, her valley. She had returned. She was back on the land where she was raised, under the sky she played, and by the river from which she drank since she was in her mother's womb.

Days before the move, Mabel went without sleeping as she tried to imagine what the valley would look like after four years. She found that only a small part of her imagination was wrong. Most of the things had stayed the same. Baliem Valley was still green and fresh. Its sky was solid blue. Its river was lazy and cool. Mabel spent almost a week looking at the sky, at the river, and walking around barefoot. She was very happy.

Moving was a little uncomfortable for the de Wissels. The house they lived in was more modest, and hot during the day because of the zinc-sheet roof. There were fewer shops compared to Manokwari. When Mrs. Hermione complained there was no bakery, Mr. de Wissel said it was because the city was developing. Fortunately, Ann and Vic, their son born in Manokwari, were happy and excited as always. "Maybe they have turned into Papuan kids who don't complain about the hot weather and the absence of a bakery," Mabel whispered to herself one afternoon as Mrs. Hermione whined about the hot weather while her children happily played in the backyard.

Mabel seemed a lot more mature in her attitude and appearance than four years earlier. She tried to grow her hair long like the girls in Manokwari. This resulted in her hair growing into a frizzy pile she had to tie down with a bandana or small ribbon. Even so, she looked sweet and very modern, especially with her dress, belt, and white shoes. Had she still lived with her tribe, she would not have dressed like that. She would be married and have a child in her arms and a pig in her noken by now. Her love of reading made her mature and modern attitude grow stronger. As she got better in Dutch and Indonesian, she often borrowed thin books with interesting covers and pictures inside from Mr. de Wissel's bookshelf. Mrs. Hermione let her teach Ann the alphabet.

Mrs. Hermione and Mr. de Wissel supported Mabel's interest in books. They gave her more free time on the weekend and let her spend it reading in the front bedroom or on the porch. But when she asked Mr. de Wissel to send her to school after she met a Papuan man who taught village children and got her interested in going to school, he refused.

Mr. de Wissel explained, "You have more than enough knowledge, Annabel. You have gone so far from the old you. If you want, you can learn more from reading. You're a smart girl, Annabel. You learn things fast, no matter what, including from books. Why go to school, especially the one for village kids we have here? It's only for those who don't know how to read and write."

"Your master is correct, dear Annabel," said Mrs. Hermione. "You're smarter. And what's important is you are happy for that, aren't you?"

Mabel nodded quietly.

"What else are you searching for? You can read, write, and count. You know Dutch and Indonesian. You're very good at cooking, babysitting, housekeeping, and gardening. What more do you want?" She touched Mabel's sad shoulders.

"We learn things to help us live, Annabel," she continued, "and you know more than enough. No need to learn unnecessary things because they will only make you suffer. Yes, suffer for being too clever, for knowing too much. Have you heard of anyone who suffers like that, Annabel? No? Very well then, I'll tell you. This kind of person lives in despair because their brain forces their body to work harder than it should. It's against nature. And when they can no longer control it, they feel defeated, disappointed, and finally, they are the most miserable people in the world. Isn't it horrible?

"Be grateful for your present condition, Annabel. Don't think too much. Just live the life you have. My husband and I only want the best for you. Trust me."

Mrs. Hermione ended her talk with a promise to teach Mabel modern medicine and nursing. She said she was a nurse in the military before she got married.

"We are women, Annabel. We can't carry the world on our shoulders. You should be happy if you can do your best for your share in this life. Women will never be men. And always remember that women can't carry the world, Annabel. Never."

Mrs. Hermione never knew that what she said that night ignited Mabel's spirit to continue studying and learning. Two years later, the de Wissels had to return to the Netherlands. On one cold foggy morning, Mabel saw them leave with the magical, giant iron bird, which she had learned was an airplane.

"I will be just fine without them."

Mabel and I indeed face this life together, and hopefully we'll always be until the day we die.

Chapter 7

KWEE

Every old person is nostalgic about their past, telling stories as they try to find a warm trace of old time glory. Mabel, however, doesn't drag her past into the present. She only tells me what is necessary. She is closer to Pum so he knows everything about her. She's not that clear with me, even when it's about an incident or someone's name. What I know about her comes from Pum, not her.

Mabel wants to hide something. And I'm curious. What made her past so dark? What happened that was so horrible it's best forgotten, just like for Mace?

Lately, Mabel hasn't been home. Pum and she go out during the day and only return, looking very tired, when the night has chased the day out of the sky.

"Where have you been, Mabel? Why did you take Pum?" Leksi asks the question for two days in a row. Left by herself, she is lonely. I sense her curiosity because I am curious as well and start guessing where they go because Mabel's answers are quite mysterious.

"Nowhere, child. Just taking care of business. Nothing important. Don't worry. I just visit with a friend to share stories. I haven't seen her for a while. Next time, I'll take you and Kwee."

Mabel is lying. Leksi and I know right away.

***

(*Mabel acts mysterious for the third day*) "Kwee, what if we just follow Mabel tomorrow? I'll pretend to go to school, but only walk as far as the market. When the sun is high enough, I'll go back home and hide in Yosi's house. Right after Mabel leaves, come and get me, and we'll follow them. From far away so Pum won't know. Will you?"

Of course, my dear Leksi. You can always count on me. That's how I would answer her, but I don't need to say it. We understand each other beyond words.

The next day, we follow Mabel and Pum as planned. When they walk straight, we do. When they cross the street, we quickly do the same. We actually took the path to the market.

Is Mabel going to the market? I don't think so. And I am right. Her long strides do not slow or stop until she passes the overcrowded parking lot and the row of vegetable vendors on the sidewalk. For a moment or two,

Mabel and Pum disappear in the crowd in front of the market. But I manage to find them even though they have gotten ahead already. Unfortunately, right at that moment I lose Leksi.

No one knows why she always gets herself into trouble. It's usually caused by her stubbornness or curiosity. After searching around, I find her with a dark-skinned shabby young man slumped in front of a closed shop. The empty green beer bottles scattered around him make me nervous. Judging by the shorts and big leather shoes he wears, the young man is an immigrant. The ugly purple noken and the necklace with a swine tooth medallion on his chest give away his identity. He is a Komen.

"Kwee, I know this man. He took my picture. He has a nice cellphone. Let's ask him to take your picture too." Without any hesitation, Leksi approaches the man.

Awakened by the sound of our steps, he stretches his dirty body like he just woke up from a long, tiring pass-out. As we get closer to him, the smell of alcohol and vomit grows stronger and reveals what has really been going on.

Leksi stops. "I think he's drunk, Kwee. We'd better leave. He might hit us."

I gladly accept her idea. My Leksi is truly smart. Approaching a drunken person is the same as trying to catch an angry, wounded swine. Dangerous. Both can easily misunderstand your good intentions. We were too late.

"Please, little sister. I'm not drunk anymore. I just want to go home, but I have no money. Can you spare some?" the man said in a hoarse voice.

I want to tell Leksi not to trust him because he might be lying, but when I look at her, I know she has already made up her mind.

She shakes her little head, moving the two braids she wears. She tells him she doesn't have any money, not even a penny.

During the following silence, it was as if the conversation never happens. The man is busy flicking dirt from his body while coughing endlessly. He seems to have guessed Leksi's answer and doesn't bother to confirm it.

Leksi stares at his purple noken like she is trying to find out what was inside.

"You had a nice cellphone that day. Where is it? Can I look at it? I just want to see my picture. Oh, and if possible, Kwee would like to have his picture taken too."

"Oh, that cellphone," the man coughed again. "I don't have it anymore. I sold it."

Leksi's eyes open wide with surprise. Her expression quickly changes to regret when she continues, "Why did you sell it? What happened to my picture? Who bought it? Was it the Regent?"

"I don't know," he smiles. "I don't know the man. He just passed by. I had no money so I had to sell my cellphone."

"No money?" Leksi frowns. "Did you have to pay your debt? Or school registration fee?"

94

The man smiles again and this time it looks more like a sour grin. He awkwardly pushes the green bottles aside and staggers to his feet. Instead of walking toward us—maybe he knows how bad he smells or as an answer to Leksi's question—he turns away and says goodbye. He says he has to be home before dark.

"Do you live nearby? You said you had no money, so how are you going home?"

"Don't worry. I still have my clothes and shoes to sell."

That noon, Leksi teaches me a lesson. "Kwee, one day we might go far away. We should take everything in the closet. If we have no money to come home, we can sell it."

***

(*Fourth day of Mabel acting mysterious*) I stay with Leksi as she finishes her breakfast and I hear a noise outside. We are in the kitchen and I don't know why there is such a ruckus. But we soon find out someone is spreading news about war on the main street. The women are asked to stay inside and keep the children safe.

Mace screams in panic before she rushes to close the windows and doors. She tells Leksi not to go to school, which makes Leksi happy.

I know Leksi doesn't remember her alphabet. "Kwee, what letter comes after V? Is it W or U? I forget what the teacher said, or I was absent when they went through it," she says between bites of steamed taro and completely ignoring my hungry glances at her plate.

The truth is I have never seen a war. It's only natural for me to want to know what exactly is happening on the main street. What is a war? Is it like Mother said, arrows pouring from the sky like rain and battle cries that summon lightning? More than that, I want to know if the war has anything to do with Mabel.

A rumor traveling from one mama to another, from the porch to the field and the market, says that Mabel is up to no good with her mysterious trips. She is supposedly attending secret meetings for an evil plan.

The mamas say, "A long time ago, Mabel was arrested. That means she's not a good person. If she goes to secret gatherings, we can be sure it's not for something good."

Honestly, I don't believe it right away. As far back as I remember, no stranger ever came to our house and arrested Mabel. If they are referring to the man dressed in white with a big bag, then it is slander. He came to check the mosquito larvae in our well and gave Mabel a pack of powder with strong smell.

Besides, there's no way the kindhearted Mabel will help commit a crime like the war. What's in it for her? In fact, she can't leave the house to sell her pinang on the sidewalk because of the war. Mace can't sell the harvest from Mabel's field at the market. I have no idea how we will later buy soap and salt because those things don't grow in our field. I also don't know where Mabel will find the money to pay the rent. The landlord, an immigrant with gold teeth, refuses to be paid with a big cluster of bananas and fat petatas. "If I accept your vegetables and fruit as payment, you should accept living in a cardboard house on a small patch of land," he scoffs.

My prejudices about Mabel mess with my head all day. Her calm behavior doesn't help either. She is such a contrast to Mace who keeps peeping nervously through a gap in the wall.

Everyone knows Mabel hates the gold company located at the end of the main street. She makes bitter remarks when talking about it. "If a dog is faithful to its master and a cat to its house, that company at the end of the street is only faithful to our gold. They don't care if they ruin the land, water, and people here as long as they get the gold. They grow rich and leave us poor in our own land."

Pum tells me about Mabel's hatred of the gold company. He said Mabel blames the company for her family's fate. Here's what he says to me:

Kwee, don't think that Mabel has always suffered. That's not true. She was happy before. One of those moments was when she got married for the second time to Pace Mauwe, a handsome man from the Amungme tribe. At that time, the tribes were not getting along and had conflicts about almost everything. Because they loved each other so much, Mabel and Pace Mauwe survived every obstacle. They were married, had their own house, and a firstborn son named Johanis.

For the first three years of their marriage, that family was living in complete peace and happiness. I never heard them argue, let alone fight.

Mabel understood her duties as a wife and did everything the best she could. She took care of her house, her husband, Johanis, and their fields. She always made time to knit a new noken, weave baskets, and never let the sago container get empty.

Pace Mauwe was a responsible, loving, and caring husband. He was a hardworking man and an agile hunter. He once went to school for a short while. He could read and count, and that attracted Mabel to him. Not many people knew numbers back then, let alone letters. Unfortunately, their happy time didn't last long.

The gold company owned by the immigrants evicted Pace Mauwe's village from the mountain slope that had been their home for so long. They provided a new village and houses as a substitute, but it was very far from the forest and especially the river. Kwee, you may not believe me when I say the forest doesn't produce sago anymore, and the river is full of the company's waste. One morning the villagers found many dead fish floating on the river. They scooped and grilled them, but Mabel showed no interest. She said those fish died of illness and anyone who ate them would share the same fate; they would get sick and die. Pace Mauwe was mad for the very first time. He no longer had a field to work on and hadn't tasted meat for a long time.

Things became worse ever since, Kwee. Many times Mabel didn't have anything to cook, and their malnourished stomachs grew bigger.

Fortunately, one day, Pace Mauwe came home with good news. The gold company had hired him. He was happy even though he only worked as a janitor. He felt like a real man again, Kwee, because he could provide for his family.

Mabel and Johanis had a good meal with his first paycheck. But guess what they ate afterward—only grilled sago or boiled taro, if there was any.

The paychecks changed Pace Mauwe. He liked to drink and stay out until late. People said he went to have fun with a woman called Fair Leg at a bar.

Mabel caught him once. She scolded him and dragged him home.

But Pace Mauwe was ungrateful. He hit Mabel and little Johanis. From then on, Kwee, Mabel's life turned more miserable.

Pace Mauwe refused to change and instead, tortured his wife and son even more. In the end, they decided to leave. Mabel rented a house. Yes, they were poor, but happy because no one hurt them anymore.

I guess the fighting on the main street has to do with the gold company. That's why, for a moment, I suspect Mabel to have something to do with it.

***

(*The next day*) I am wrong. I'll apologize to Mabel when I have the opportunity. I'll even kiss her *galangal*-like thumb if I have to. Thank goodness, Pum doesn't know about my prejudice yesterday. If he knew, he would go on and on about how I must be a good, positive thinking pig.

It turns out Mabel has nothing to do with the war that continues to rage on the main street. This morning, news came to our house. The mama messenger says the war is a fight between the highland and lowland tribes. Mabel comes from neither of these.

Thank goodness. I'm even more convinced that Mabel is a good person. The rumor about someone as sweet as her is too horrible to be true. I don't trust any rumor easily.

***

(*The day after*) The war continues. Mabel, Mace, Leksi, Pum, and I remain trapped in our cramped little house. We have more than enough food in the kitchen so we won't starve—who knows when the war will stop?

Don't those who fight in the war have to eat? Who prepares their food?

After I finish my food, I brace myself to peep on the situation outside. I play deaf when Mace warns me about being stabbed in the eye by a stray arrow getting in through the large crack. But before I can look through the crack, someone bangs on the door. The mama messenger pays us another visit.

Mace rushes to greet our guest. "Anything new?"

"How many are dead?" Mabel is right behind Mace.

The mama messenger, with probing eyes, readied herself to do her job of spreading the news that she got somewhere, somehow. She moves from one neighbor to another for nothing but the pride of being the center of attention. Under normal conditions, her presence only brings cheap rumors instead of reliable news. She also spends most of her time at some nosy mama's place. On the flip side, when no one dares to go out, her presence can bring the good news we are waiting for: the war has ended.

The mama messenger is awesome. She is like a storyteller who bewitches anyone with her words, which are simple but sound so amazing from her thick lips. She can also say a very long line with one breath, just like she is doing right now. It turns out the two tribes are fighting over the border of their gold mining areas on the river. The highland tribe believes the lowlanders have secretly moved their border and left them the landslide-prone area. As a result, four days ago a miner from the highlanders died in a landslide while doing his job.

"Can't they use their brains? They kill each other over the outsider's fault."

"Whose fault, Mabel?" Leksi, who listens to the mama messenger's story in amazement, suddenly asks.

"None other but the gold company. They're like that, child, always causing trouble. They always lie here and there. They make our people fight among ourselves. Some of us died, got sick, and became poor and miserable. They just want our gold, Leksi. They don't care if we struggle to live or even die."

"Shh, Mabel. Lower your voice, please."

Mace glances around the house and at the ceiling before her worried eyes finally land on the mama messenger in front of her.

"I can't, Lisbeth. This is how I speak," Mabel stubbornly answered.

"Fine. Do as you want."

Like always, Mace gives in when she has to deal with Mabel's stubbornness. However, she can't hide the worry in her eyes as she notices how the mama messenger seems restless.

I sense what Mace is thinking. She is afraid the mama messenger will use Mabel's words for her next gossip with the neighbors. We will soon find out if Mace's suspicions are true.

The mama messenger says goodbye and leaves in a hurry, but the slowly closing door enables us to catch a particular look in her eyes and a half-formed smile on her lips.

Chapter 8

LEKSI

I want to play with Yosi longer. We have exciting games we haven't played, but Mama Helda's yelling is too loud to ignore. Yosi cringes like she feels her mother pulling her ears.

"I need to go." She walks away, then smiles and waves goodbye.

I try not to stop my best friend with words that will only make her sadder. While I untie the jump rope from the pinang tree by the fence, I give her a sorry look. It's hard for her to leave our game of Karet Merdeka. She almost won the last jump. More than that, I know Yosi shares my feeling. After being locked in the house for more than a week because of the war, being able to play outside again feels like a dream come true.

"Good news. The war is over. Both sides lost the same number of men, ten highlanders and ten lowlanders," said Mama Mote, the mama messenger, when she came yesterday. She showed up with shiny eyes and mixed feelings: happy, relieved, and miserable at the same time because it meant that her visits won't be needed anymore.

I played house by myself under the table. Mace said we had to keep our doors and windows closed all the time to make sure the danger stayed outside, so I pretended that a war had also happened in my imaginary world. I hid under the table where the hanging ends of the stiff and dirty tablecloth protected me like walls of a castle. I stayed there until the mama messenger sat on a wooden chair in front of me and began to talk with nonstop excitement.

"The main street is empty and the corpses have been cleared. There are only pools of blood, arrows, and wooden sticks on the ground. A few armed guards are in place just in case something happens. Those who died were still young."

Mama Mote muttered to herself, saying she would go to the hospital to find out about the poor kids. Maybe she could help deliver the bad news to their family. She kept going until Mabel interrupted.

"Meanwhile, Papua lost another twenty brainless people. Brave but stupid men who were easily poisoned to kill their own brothers. They died so young over something so trivial. When will these people realize…."

Mama Mote answered Mabel with silence. From under the table, I saw her hand reaching down. She'd rather scratch the scabies on her calf until there were long white lines than comment on what Mabel said. But a reaction came from another direction in a form of a loud sigh. I turned my head and watched Mace's feet with their cracked soles that reminded me of dry ground. The sound must have come from her. I knew her well enough that I could imagine how she frowned when worried. I never know why she behaves like that every time Mabel says things I can't understand. She acted like Mabel had let out a big secret that would put us in danger if someone found out. I did the same when Yosi accidentally spilled our secret to Karel that I had found a treasure in the field. But usually Mabel didn't seem to care that much.

In the next minute, Mace stomped to the kitchen. She came back soon afterward and talked politely.

"Please have some pinang, Mama Mote."

She tried to swallow her anger in front of her guest.

Just like how kids were not allowed to talk about any ghost or spirit they saw so as not to be possessed, the talk switched from war to the price of things. Mace gave her opinion that we should raise the price of pinang since other things were already getting more expensive. Meanwhile, I got bored playing alone and decided to end my imaginary war to go to Yosi's house.

"Leksi, where are you going? Can't you see that no one is out on the street?" Mace's warning stopped me. My smile turned into a frown. I really wanted to play. I tried to sulk for a few seconds, hoping she would let me go outside. It didn't work.

"You can play tomorrow. I'm sure Yosi isn't allowed out today. Try to be patient, Leksi. Tomorrow you can play all you want until late."

That's what Mace promised me yesterday, but Mama Helda didn't make the same promise to Yosi. I'm saying this because when we met again, Yosi must make dinner for her family like she did every day.

"Leksi!" Yosi's loud yell startled me, and woke me from my daydreaming. I saw her skinny figure near her porch. With one hand waving, Yosi mouthed words. She tried to send me a silent message from far away. Too bad I couldn't understand what she said. Somehow I was sure she made a promise to play together tomorrow. I answered her with a big grin. It was the right answer because I saw her start to smile. Her look of fear returned when Mama Helda's yelling came thundering from inside the house, "Yosi, move it, or do you want me to hit you?"

***

I can't wait to finish my class today. I think about which exciting games I'll play with Yosi later. But when I get home and tell her the choice I made before the school bell rang, she tells me her mother won't let her play. She has to take care of Kaye, her sick youngest brother.

"Kaye has a fever, Leksi. Mama told me to take care of him and not to leave the house, let alone play."

I should have known. Kaye has shown signs of coming down with a fever since early morning. He was so cranky that I woke earlier than normal. His yelling made the roosters crow before they saw the sun. Dogs barked too. Meanwhile, Mabel washed our clothes by the well and guessed at the reason for Kaye's painful crying.

"Was he beaten or did he fall? Or maybe accidentally squashed in the door?"

Before I leave for school, I see Yosi sweeping the yard. "Yosi, are we going to play later?"

"You bet, Leksi," she answers. "You decide what game we'll play."

She doesn't expect her mother to give her the duty of caring for her sick brother. When I ask about Kaye, she cheerfully says, "It's just a fever, but my mama is taking care of him. She might not go to the field today."

Kaye is only three but he acts like a giant baby. He cries and sulks too easily. Even Mama Helda can't stand his crankiness.

Yosi is very patient and caring. She never pinches or scolds Kaye when he acts up. She talks to him, buys him candy when she has money, or lets him interrupt her game.

"We'll play when Kaye is well. I'm sure his fever will be gone by tomorrow," Yosi says before Kaye's crying calls her back into the house.

I thought I would be angry all day because my plan to play with Yosi fell through, but that old woman came at the right moment. It was almost noon and I was very bored playing with dirt by myself.

Our guest was Mabel's. She arrived from Biak. When they meet, the two old ladies shout greetings and hug with tears running down their cheeks for quite a while.

Mabel introduces her as her oldest best friend, but the guest corrects her, saying that she isn't a relative who has gone without seeing Mabel for a long time. Her name is Mama Kori.

"This is my granddaughter. Leksi," Mabel said, introducing me.

"Leksi? My, my, what a sweet girl. Really sweet." She praises me in her warm voice and pinches me lovingly in the cheek. I give her my most perfect smile, a smile that gradually fades when she continues with a question to Mabel, "Is she Johanis' daughter?"

"Yes. That's her."

"Oh, no wonder. She has his eyes. And his nose too."

As she says this, I touch my eyes and nose. Are they like his? In what way? At this moment, I want to run to the mirror in the bedroom and see and enjoy what is alike in our faces—father's and mine—the way Mama Kori says, because I have never seen his face. I find it really hard to leave the living room. I want to hear the many new things from our guest. I decide to check in the mirror later and stay on Mace's lap. Mabel introduces her as Johanis' wife.

"Lisbeth." Mace says her name as she politely shakes our guest's hand.

At noon, our house is more cheerful than usual. Not only does Mama Kori bring many souvenirs, she also has stories that make us laugh, although some of them surprise me.

Mama Kori tells about how naughty my father was as a child, including the time they had to take him to the clinic because a goose had pecked his butt. She makes Mabel blush when she tells the story of the charming young man who came to Mabel's house every day, bringing her the harvest from his field.

"You know, Leksi, that young man was crazy about your Mabel. Back then she was the most beautiful of all. Nobody could compete with her."

"Really?"

Mama Kori says like it's just us: "Believe me, child." She throws a glance at Mabel, who shouts in return.

"Ah, Kori. Come on, just stop this story."

"No way, Annabel. Your granddaughter must know a little about her grandmother's past." She continues: "Just so you know, Leksi, before those wrinkles appeared, your Mabel glowed in beauty like you. Yes, just like you."

Hearing that, my chest puffs proudly and I smile. Being praised like that by someone I just met was different from being praised by Mabel or Mace. My smile faded in the next second and it was gone completely when I thought about something.

"Mama Kori, will there be a young man coming here every day, bringing me the harvest from his field?"

Again, laughter fills our cramped house, right when Mace finishes placing lunch on the table.

"Let us eat, Mama."

"Thank you, Lisbeth."

Pum shows up out of nowhere and Mama Kori recognizes him right away. "My goodness, Pum. Is that really you? Looks like we've both grown old."

This day, lunch is a lot merrier than usual.

PUM

Don't ask why Mama Kori gives me such a warm welcome. Of course, she heard about me from Mabel. Her house used to be next to Mabel's old rented house in a different housing complex. Mabel thinks of Mama Kori as the sister she never had. She helped Mabel when she needed a place to regain her strength and spirit after leaving Pace Mauwe. She stayed by Mabel when she had a big misfortune that forced her to leave little Johanis. And she tells this story to Leksi, Mace, and Kwee. If not for her, they will never hear this, especially because Mabel keeps it a secret from everyone except me. I agree with what she said earlier.

"You are too introverted, Annabel, even with your own grandchildren. I don't think there's anything wrong with letting the young learn from our past. Who knows? Maybe there's something they can fix or use as an example."

Mama Kori took us back a few decades, to a time that was most difficult for Mabel or, I believe, any human. This is how she starts her story:

"Humans will always be humans. They aren't angels. They make mistakes and they sin. Don't ever doubt the story I'm about to tell you. If you do, one day the same thing may happen to you.

"I visited Mabel that day to help her take care of Johanis who had a fever after getting pricked by a nail in his foot. She was in the kitchen cooking, when they came:

mean-looking men in uniform with weapons on their shoulders. They looked like cowards, and were loud and rude like thugs instead of educated people. They yelled at us and were so offensive. One man in the front said they were looking for Annabel Okale and wanted to take her to their place.

"I asked them politely and without prejudice, 'What for? Must you do it now? Her son is sick.' Do you know what I got for an answer? Yelling and a string of curses. They pushed me and I fell between their mighty boots that walked all over her house. I could only look when those boots started to act as they wished. They roamed without permission, kicking the furniture as if it would put up a fight. They broke the only divan after they moved Johanis to my lap. They probably thought Mabel was hiding under it. Oh, what a stupid thing to do. Really stupid. Even a child knows how to behave in someone's home. Not them. Their uniforms and weapons made them lose their morality.

"God forgive, I thought only animals were dragged from the woods after the hunters caught them. But a person can be treated the same way. So cruel, especially when the person was innocent, and Mabel was completely innocent.

"I've tried to erase that day from my memory, but I can't. It's really hard. It even gives me nightmares and brings me to tears. Imagine a mother being forced to leave her house by brute force right in front of her toddler. I watched them and held little Johanis, who wouldn't stop crying. Two men dragged Mabel like a bag of sand from the kitchen to the front door.

"Mabel looked like a wounded animal ready to die for her freedom. That's right. She looked just like one. She fought with all her might, ignoring how they tore her clothes. She howled her protest and tried to free herself from the fingers that sank deep into her flesh. She screamed, asking them why they treated her so bad. Mabel had never stolen or done anything bad, let alone harmed anyone. And do you know the answer she got? A kick at her hips, a slap on her cheek, and yelling telling her to shut up. Poor Mabel. I screamed hysterically as I could not bear to watch what was happening."

Mama Kori stops here. She leaves her story hanging. The gray-haired woman freezes in silence, as if to hold back something powerful inside her. But she fails.

"I don't think I can take anymore. I really can't." In front of the five of us, she sobs like a child who has lost her toys. She looks miserable.

Ah, tears. I realize there is a fine line between sadness and guilt. It's as fine as the film that glazes over your eyes when you cry about those two things. It's so fine that anyone who cries out of guilt can choose to say the tears are of sadness.

Mama Kori isn't the only one who cries. I too cry, although inside. I don't know why but I believe our sadness might come from the same place—our inability to help Mabel that day. I feel guilty about not being able to stop those armed men from taking her away, but I wasn't born yet.

The men took Mabel and locked her up in a place that, according to the rumor, was like hell on earth. They had all kinds of tortures they did to her over and over, ignoring how she begged for them to stop. I keep imagining her being somewhere as horrible as that.

Mama Kori no longer cried and prepared herself to continue the story. During the remainder of the story, I was overcome by guilt over the incident. I listened, anxiously.

"I swear to God, Mabel was innocent. I believed that before she said so. I never doubted it. People said she was accused of being involved in the rebellion, and had hidden some of the runaway rebels.

"I said, 'There's no way Annabel Okale would do such thing. I know her very well. No stranger ever spends a night at her house or pays her a visit. All she does is take care of her son and her field, and sell the harvested crops at the market. Other than that, she stays home to weave baskets and knit nokens.'

"I said this loudly in front of the villagers who gossiped after Mabel's arrest. Among the crowd was a military official with a thick mustache. On the third day after they dragged Mabel away, his men brought me to him.

"Yes, I was arrested too. Being forced to visit them was more like it, since I spent only one day inside. They just wanted to ask me about Mabel. I immediately went with great hope the information I had would free my poor friend right away. I was wrong. It turned out those men in uniform often tricked their prey to willingly enter a trap. And the bastards tricked me.

"From morning until night, they forced me to answer a series of strange questions. I had no idea how they had anything to do with me. When I answered 'I don't know' or 'What do you mean?' I was tortured again. My God, I wished I could die. Even if I ended up in hell, at least God would have only given me a fair share of torture based on my sins. Doesn't the Bible say so? But I was trapped in a place where these uniformed men—who I believed were well educated—had gathered. They tortured me endlessly without any reason other than that I didn't know the answer or understand the question. My mistake wasn't unforgiveable, was it? They had forgotten that only God is mighty."

We are silent as Mama Kori's voice trails off. She looks at the floor with tears streaming down her face. I suppose she feels the pain all over again. Mabel looks stronger although tears well in her eyes. Slowly, the fingers on her crooked left hand reach for Mama Kori's hand on the table. She holds tightly as if trying to share her strength. The room is in complete silence as Mama Kori cries quietly.

The torture Mama Kori suffered was much lighter than what Mabel had to bear. I'm certain of this because on one cold night, Mabel shared her painful experience with me:

"Johanis was asleep. I just finished applying herbal ointment on my wounds. It was one week after I had returned home. After being under arrest for two weeks, I showed up at the front yard looking like a zombie. I must have smelled horrible and I knew I was extremely filthy. I had wounds, bruises, swellings, and dry blood all over my body. My son barely recognized me.

"At first I wanted nobody but God to know what I went through, Pum, but I needed to let it out. I couldn't hold it inside me. I've tried so many times to find the answer to why I was tortured, but I haven't found it. The only reason that keeps on running inside my head is that I was tortured because I'm a nobody.

"You know, Pum, that place made me realize some people want to play God. They create this little world for them to rule. Their words are the commands. Their weapon is the devil's whip that's also the kiss of the angel of death, and can cripple you for the rest of your life or take your life away. Their uniforms serve as cloaks to hide their devious acts. The devilish acts they hide behind their so-called bravery. That place was really hell on earth.

"Pum, would you believe me if I told you they can make you look guilty or innocent? They have so many ways to make you confess to doing something so bad that it's unforgivable for seven generations to come. I experienced that myself."

Mabel told me about the wounds and bruises on her body, and what caused them. Only then did I learn how horribly they had treated her. It was worse than what a drunken paitua would do to a scabbed, limping old dog. He would do nothing more than kick it, throw stones at it, or occasionally take a pee on it.

She said that on her first day, they started to beat, kick, and slap her so she would admit doing something she never did. They questioned her for hours and hours without a toilet break, let alone a meal. When they didn't get the confession they wanted, they put her in a tiny cell with hardly any ventilation and a floor full of human waste that had been there for days.

"That cell stunk so terribly that I thought I would die of air poisoning once I set foot in it. Can you imagine that, Pum? They refused to go near it themselves. They just pointed their guns at me and told me to go in. I no longer felt I was human. I was not even a pig that loved a dirty sty. In their eyes, I was lower than any animal on earth. I was so low that I only deserved to sleep in waste. I do believe they were heartless."

A few uniformed men in masks interrogated her in the room. They forced her to answer a series of questions. When she answered, "I don't know," or "I never knew that person," they kicked her in the head until she fell to the floor.

"I honestly didn't know the man they were looking for, Pum. I had never heard his name until then. I only knew his mother. She happened to be looking for chayote seeds, so I went to her house twice to bring her the best quality seeds. I learned her name from a customer at the market who turned out to be her relative. The house down below was where the old woman and her son they accused of rebellion had lived. Just because I went there twice to sell seeds, I was arrested for helping them. Hah! What kind of law is that?"

Mabel then told me about the day they made her meet other people who were also arrested and said to be helping the rebels, including the old woman. Mable paused many times along that story because she kept crying. She told me about the horrible torture she had to endure that day. Four fingers on her left hand were permanently deformed because they were squashed under the foot of a table where a fat officer was sitting. Not only that, she was forced to witness their other cruel acts.

"They regarded the rebels and anyone who knew them as animals instead of humans, Pum. But animals don't deserve to be treated with such cruelty. They didn't show any mercy at all. Maybe their hearts had turned to stone. They enjoyed burning a prisoner's skin with cigarettes, and laughed while slamming a prisoner's hand in the door. But their rudest act was when they stuffed the old woman's mouth with their socks before slapping her until she passed out. A woman like her gave birth to them. Where did they come from to make them act like that?"

It was almost dark when Mama Kori came to this part of the story. Mabel told Mama Kori about that dark period in her life a couple of months later. The suffering they experienced is one of the ties that hold them together, and keep their friendship strong even when they don't seen each other for decades. They each had solved one of life's puzzles.

"Understand this, child. Fear is the beginning of foolishness. And foolishness—don't ever take it lightly—can make anyone regard others as less than a human." Mama Kori finishes her story and looks around the room before she rests her gaze on Leksi. "That's why, Leksi, you must promise me to study hard and become a clever child who will make your Mace and Mabel proud. Will you?"

Leksi nodded eagerly.

I caught a sparkle in her eyes, the same sparkle Mabel showed back then when she realized that the end of one thing could mean the beginning of another.

"The ground is always muddier at the end of a long rainy season, Pum. But if we work hard, there will be more petatas to plant and harvest later. I can't just give up. I can't."

Chapter 9

KWEE

Like me, Leksi has never liked Pace *Poro Boku*, Yosi's father. He's not a nice person. He likes to curse, throw things, threaten others with arrows, and gets upset without any good reason. It's almost impossible to talk things through with him and he gets offended pretty quick. His lips are so thick that he seems to pout all the time. Few neighbors can stand talking to him for very long.

"When he speaks, spit comes out of his mouth like rain," Leksi explains to Karel when he asks why he hardly ever sees Yosi's father talking to other paces.

Pace Poro Boku gets drunk so often that his body reeks of alcohol. Looking at his constantly red and teary eyes, anyone can see he's never well. He's either drunk or in a bad mood. Just like this morning.

"I only asked for Yosi, but he told me to leave right away," Leksi tells Mace, who sees her off to school at the fence.

"Maybe you asked impolitely."

"But I was polite, Mace."

"Or maybe you greeted him too loud and woke him up."

"No, he wasn't asleep. He was sitting on the porch."

If Mabel didn't return from doing the laundry, that debate would go on and on. Mabel carries a blue pail of clean, lemon-scented clothes ready to be hung on the clotheslines. She starts her routine a little late this morning because she chooses to keep Mama Kori company until her son picks her up. Mama Kori is scheduled to return to Biak at noon.

"Cut it out, no more. Don't talk about your neighbor. You had best go to school, Leksi. Study well. Don't go to Yosi's house to play today," she said, glancing at our neighbor's empty porch.

Mabel's words spark endless questions from Leksi. She threatens to skip school if no one tells her where Yosi is. "She said she would play with me today. She said Kaye would be fine because it is just a fever. Is Kaye worse? Or is Yosi sick too?"

"No, Leksi. Kaye is fine and so is Yosi."

"Then why won't Yosi come out and meet me? Why didn't she sweep her front yard this morning? Is she home?"

"No, she's not home."

"Where did she go? Who will cook and keep her house?"

"Leksi, Leksi."

If only she knew what happened the night before, a couple of hours after she fell asleep to Mama Kori's story after dinner, which made her really tired and bored. Indeed, by then, Mama Kori talked about Mabel's change in attitude after her arrest. According to her, Mabel became quiet and careful. Mabel didn't want to give the uniformed men any reason to arrest her again.

"It doesn't mean Mabel turned into a coward. In fact, she voices her opinion loudly if she thinks she's right. She told me that she felt stupid to fear those armed men in uniform. Just like her, they are only humans who will die when their time comes," Mama Kori, ended her story last night while Leksi was fast asleep on Mabel's lap.

The gossip that the villagers spread about Mabel before the war broke turned out to be true. Just like what Mama Kori told us, Mabel was arrested once. Hearing this from her didn't cause the hard feelings or embarrassment I felt when I heard it from the people who talked behind Mabel's back. Listening to Mama Kori's explanation, the newspaper should write about Mabel's story so many more people will talk about it. What happened to her is not right and needs some clarification to clear her reputation.

Everyone awake in the living room knew there was a fight at Yosi's house. We heard a man's angry voice, and the sounds of falling and crashing. Without pressing their ears to the door's crack and windows, Mabel and Mace guessed what started the fight. The same as every fight before. Yosi's drunken father came home angry and beat his wife over small matters. In the dead of the night, his rage was loud and clear. He kept shouting, asking for money, and we didn't hear his wife's answer. Something was slammed and shattered before we heard a woman scream in pain. All the noises seemed to go on and on.

Mabel, Mama Kori, and Mace exchanged meaningful glances in silence. They tried to carry on with their stories and it didn't last long. The silence overcame them, an awkward one. Anyone with good hearing wouldn't be able to ignore that fight. How could you? The house is right beside ours. They're our closest neighbor. Their daughter and Leksi are best friends. But we couldn't do anything because it's not our business, it's theirs.

Mabel broke the silence after the fight ended with Yosi's mother screaming for mercy. "The woman is the victim in any fight. Whether right or wrong, she's always the one who suffers."

Mama Kori let out a deep sigh. "You're right, Mabel. Women's fate has stayed the same. We are too stupid to fight and too afraid to protest. And so it goes. We live in misery created by our husbands. We are slaves until death sets us free."

Mace asked, "Are all women destined to that kind of life?"

"No, Lisbeth," said Mabel. "Only a fool believes that. Those women won't try to find a better life, both physically and mentally. The arrogant men think they have power and are better than women. The fools also include those who claim to protect and respect women

122

but don't appreciate the things women do, let alone the things we say."

"What Mabel says is absolutely right, child. Fate is a blank map and you alone set the course according to what you want to achieve in life. You get a bad ending when you're not careful."

That line from Mama Kori ended the conversation. What I hear afterward is the noise of table and chairs being moved. Mama Kori and Mabel hold each other tight as they sleep on the worn-out mat in the living room.

***

Leksi is very upset and I can't blame her. Her best friend, Yosi, has disappeared. So, everyone must grant whatever wish she has today.

"Hurry up. If you want to come along, you have to promise you'll be good," Mabel says.

"I want Kwee to come too. Can he?"

"Okay, fine. Take him with you."

That's why I'm here in the middle of a chaotic meeting.

I'm curious about this meeting. It started before the war between the tribes on the main street, or since Mabel left the house with Pum early in the morning and returned only when it was dark. Leksi and I tried to follow them and failed. The villagers' deplorable gossip got into my head and made me have bad thoughts about Mabel. I suspected her to attend some secret evil meeting. But when I stand on all fours among these people, I hear nothing evil. They just want to hold a protest.

"I've told you, let's hold a protest. Period, no need for a meeting or discussion. The company rarely listens to us. When they do, they pretend they don't understand. When we use our Papuan language, they use Indonesian. When we switch to Indonesian, they switch to a foreign language. They think we're stupid and not equal to them. A protest is better."

"True. I agree. Let's have a protest."

"Me too."

"I agree. Especially if we hold it down the main street so their cars can't pass and workers can't go to their offices. What do you think?"

"That's a good idea, a really good one. I'm all for that."

The voices fill the small living room belonging to the paitua who sells pumpkins at the market. He tries to help Mabel soothe a passionate, frizzy-haired young man. His dark face shows the rage he holds back and his eyes have a steely, piercing look. I'm sure he will go berserk soon if he doesn't simmer down.

He sells vegetables near the parking lot, and talks just as loud as when he sells his vegetables. He's that guy all right.

"Just be calm, child. Be calm. We must think everything through before committing to an action that will make others suffer losses."

"But Mabel, we have our share of loss already."

"Yes, true. Everyone knows that, but is this an excuse to make them suffer too, by blocking cars and stopping workers from entering their offices? Is there any guarantee the protest will make them buy our vegetables like they promised? What if it's the other way around? They get scared and refuse to work with us. Many immigrants think we natives are fierce and scary."

"Ah, that's it how it should be. They should be afraid of us because they are only immigrants, outsiders. They make money and live on our land. They get rich and live a good life from taking our gold. Yet we get nothing but their waste and empty promises."

The frizzy-haired young man spits on the floor to express his anger. He sits down as his friends clap and praise him for telling the truth.

A mace with breasts like papayas springs to her feet from a worn-out wooden chair in the corner of the room. With her breasts shaking and moving, she curses the company people who she regards as ungrateful. Waves of applause fill the stuffy room. The anger of the frizzy-haired young man spreads. The paituas, paces, maces, and the children voice their anger toward the company that doesn't keep the promise of buying their vegetables.

"Kwee, let's get out of here. My ears will hurt if we stay any longer." Leksi forces me to leave the public venting although I'm enjoying myself. I leave the stuffy room full of sweaty people who can't reach any decision even though night is approaching.

"No wonder Mabel doesn't talk that much, Kwee. Her friends are noisy and loud, so she must use all of her voice to quiet them. If she asks me to come along next time, I won't go. I'd rather stay home and play. Where's Yosi? Do you know, Kwee? Maybe she…."

On our way home, Leksi asks Mabel, "Mabel, besides gold, does the company also take children? I'm worried they took Yosi and hid her at the mountain at the end of the main street."

LEKSI

I really miss Yosi and it makes me so sad. I can't sleep or study. She promised we would play together, and I miss how she smiles whenever she wins. I've been quiet the past few days and prefer to stare at the fence of Yosi's house. I really wish for her to suddenly come running and say: "I'm back, Leksi. Let's play again."

For the past five days, I haven't see her skinny figure. My eyes feel hot and my body is weak. My head is full of so many things I want to tell Yosi that it feels heavy and loaded, like a small closet stuffed with unfolded clothes. So full. Mace says I am sick and she won't let me go to school. If I was healthy as usual, the news would make me jump up and down in joy. Instead, I become sadder as I lie on the bed with Pum and Kwee.

"I want to go out."

"Later, when you're well," said Mace.

"But I'm well already."

"No, you're not. You still have a fever."

"It's because I haven't showered."

"Don't argue, Leksi. Just get a lot of rest. Mabel said she'd take you to meet Yosi when you're well."

"Really?"

"Believe your Mabel. She's so worried about you being sick."

I hold on to Mace's words until I get well, and even willingly drink the nasty herbal medicine Mabel brews. It numbs my tongue for a whole day. I can't tell the sweetness of sugar from the bitter of papaya leaves. Afraid my tongue won't return to normal, I cry.

I tried to enjoy my time in bed. I played deaf when I heard Karel and other children walk pass the house, chatting cheerfully while playing *Roda Gelinding*. To cheer up, I think about the stories I want to tell Yosi. One thing for sure, I'll keep the story of Mabel's arrest to myself. I don't want Yosi to accuse me of lying.

I could tell Yosi about Mabel's friends, her fellow vegetables sellers at the market who wanted to hold a protest because the company doesn't keep its promise. The company cancelled the plan to buy vegetables from them. This is what I hear when Mabel takes me to the house of her friend, a paitua. I know him as a pumpkin seller at the market. Inside his house, Mabel and other vegetables sellers gather to talk about vegetables, a protest, and this and that. Since I'm not interested, I'm sure Yosi wouldn't be either.

I decide to tell her another story. I'll tell her about the guests who came to my house lately, bringing presents like colorful tee shirts, posters, and many stickers showing a photo of two smiling paitua.

All I knew was that those guests were looking for Mabel. They came with someone who knew her already. The guests talked like they were doing the counting in a hide and seek game. They sounded like a student reciting multiplication tables in front of the class. Every word was well prepared and they were afraid of making one mistake. From behind the wall, I heard them repeat what the people in the pumpkin seller's house said. I don't understand what it was all about. One thing is sure, they shake Mabel's hand firmly before they leave and say, "Mama, please don't forget," and mentioned the different names they want Mabel to choose at the election.

"What is the Striped Party, Mabel?" asks Leksi.

"Name of a party."

"Yes, I know. But what is a party? Why must we choose one?"

Mabel smiles before answering, "It's a group's name, Leksi."

"Like the study group at school?"

"Yes, exactly."

"But, Mabel, they're old. Why should they form a study group like us students? What else do they want to learn?"

"They want to learn how to lead the people, child."

"Meaning?"

"Ah, you can ask your questions later. Rest so you'll get well and don't think too much."

I never argue when she says that. Meeting Yosi is more important than getting more information about the guests. I'll find out eventually anyway. When I am well and can roam again, I'll eavesdrop on the mamas' gossiping from behind their fence. Lucky I don't have to wait too long. Four days later, Mace checks my temperature and happily announces my fever is gone.

"Get up a little earlier tomorrow. Mabel will take you to Yosi's place."

"What? Tomorrow? Why not today?"

"Because Mabel has something she must do now."

"Is it the protest?"

"Hush, don't be a smartass. Go and prepare the things you want to take to Yosi. Yesterday you said you had a present for her."

"I almost forgot. Thanks for reminding me, Mace. I want to give her the pink tee shirt from the Flowery Party. Can I?"

"It belongs to Mabel. Ask her later."

"Will she give me one?"

"Tell her she has many shirts from her guests. Giving up one shouldn't be a problem."

The sun shines for more hours than usual and it takes longer for night to fall. I wait at the door while the day moves like an old snail. When it's almost dark, two tired figures walk toward the porch. Mabel and Pum. My worries turn into joy instantly. I welcome them, especially Mabel. Without letting her sit, I ask if I can give the tee shirt from the Flowery Party to Yosi.

"Go ahead and choose anyone you like, child. No tee shirt, poster, or sticker can buy your Mabel. None of that free stuff can make our life better. It's just a lie."

The next morning, without bothering to understand what Mabel said, I stuff some of Mabel's free shirts and stickers into a black plastic bag. I want to give them to Yosi and her brothers. Together with Mabel and Pum, I happily walk to a place far away from home. The place that has its name on a board, the place that houses Yosi.

Chapter 10

PUM

My old-age fatigue is gone. I love smelling the colors. The colors on the flags, banners, posters, and the giveaway tee shirts. It's that time again, when many political parties spring into action with their campaign. Time really does fly. The last election seems like it was yesterday.

The big event is the election of the Regent and Vice Regent. *Pilkada* is what people call it. We never had such a thing before. This kind of campaign only happens during the general election. But what do I care? I don't have the right to vote and I'm grateful. Why? Because I don't want to be like Mabel who prepares herself to be disliked because she decides not to choose any party that tries to bribe her with tee shirts, posters, and stickers. These are the people who visited us some time ago, well-dressed men that Mabel's friends and acquaintances from the market brought over. Somehow, they thought she was the leader of the vegetables sellers, the spokeswoman to settle their problems with the gold company.

"That's why, Mama Annabel, we come to offer you a better way. Our party guarantees a win-win solution for the problems you and your friends have with the company. Our party knows certain government officials, Mama. So don't worry. Just trust us. Our party fights for the people, especially the oppressed."

That's the sweet talk I hear coming from one of the guests. The strange thing is that the guests who come later say similar things. They all promise a better solution to the problem. They know someone important. And every one takes pride in being the defender of the people. Fortunately, Mabel doesn't buy any of the talk.

"Don't they realize it's them making the people suffer more? Empty promises. Puh! Nonsense. If they really want to help, why do they ask for our support in return? Also, why do should they wait until the election is over? Do they think eating nothing will make us full?"

I don't blame Mabel for being irritated. She has been disappointed before, really disappointed. Some time ago, she placed high hopes on a leader who many believed would improve their lives. "He promises us great things. Our lives will surely prosper."

The truth was....

"Those people forgot about us once they were elected," she ranted when she realized nothing had changed after her idol became the leader.

She still rents her house from an immigrant although it's on the land of her ancestors. She has the same diet: sago, petatas, taro, and vegetables from the field. She only eats rice and meat when she has extra income or is invited to a party. She can't remember when she bought the shabby clothes she keeps in her closet. Meanwhile, close to our rundown village where many cannot afford electricity, tall steel towers begin to show up. We're still clueless about their function other than to serve as the clothesline for the maces that live in that area.

Mabel is more careful with her choices. Nice appearances and sweet promises can no longer win her over easily, let alone free stuff like giveaway tee shirts. In fact, these annoy her. Honestly, I regret Mabel's decision a little when she lets Leksi take the entire lot of giveaway tee shirts to Yosi. Not that I want one. I just imagine the sight it will make if she hangs all of them out to dry on one sunny day. Oh, it will be splendid. The barren land of ours will look more cheerful and colorful. Those strong-smelling colors can conceal the dust from the street that sticks to our walls. If only Mama Helda still lived next door. I would stare at her clothesline all the time because the tee shirts belonged to her children now, Yosi and her three brothers.

Speaking of Yosi.

A few days before, Mabel, Leksi, and I visited a safe house, that's what Mabel tells Leksi, that is located in a different residential area than ours. That was where Mama Helda and her children had taken refuge until who knows when.

I thought the fight at Yosi's house that night would end like usual; Mama Helda acting as if nothing happened the next day although her swollen and bruised face gave a different testimony. I was wrong.

What Pace Poro Boku did—pardon me for using the nickname Leksi gave Yosi's father. I simply hate him—was way out of line. Mama Helda couldn't take it anymore. In the morning, pale and sick Mama Helda tells us everything in a sad, teary voice. This was what she said:

"Mabel, let me apologize for not listening to you. You were right. Every day my husband was more violent. He took my silence as submission. He made me the target of his anger. Every time he came home drunk, he tortured me. I'm sure you heard us, right? His yelling, my screaming. Oh, Mabel, I'm so ashamed. Ashamed....

"For quite some time, I'd felt that I couldn't take it anymore. Especially when I was heavily pregnant. I couldn't stand being slapped, hit, pushed and kicked. It's as if all my bones were crushed. I tried to hold on. I thought maybe one day he would change and become the understanding man he was in the early years of our marriage. I thought if he got a raise or the kids behaved well, and everything he needed was ready without having to ask for it, he would be nicer. I was wrong. It was just a dream that will never come true."

She stops, interrupted by a heavy cough. Quickly, she places her trembling hand over her mouth. When the coughing is over, the hand stays there. The frizzy red-haired woman blinks her eyes faster to hold back her tears.

"Mabel, you once told me that we can't change someone unless they want to change. Now I see the truth. My husband thinks he never gets enough of a raise, and often uses this as an excuse to get drunk. He keeps getting angry although I always remind the kids to be good and stay quiet. Not only that, he's dissatisfied with me in bed. I do whatever he wants although sometimes it feels strange and painful—I hope you know what I mean because I'm too embarrassed to explain. Even so, I never complain or refuse. Not once, Mabel. I don't know what kind of demon got into him and made all this happen."

She drew one long heavy breath before she continued. Her face showed the pain she felt inside.

"He asked for extra money to buy more liquor, but when I said no, he finally told me the truth. He said.... He said it was for Fair Leg. He wanted to sleep with her. He had the guts to ask me for the money. Can you imagine? Bastard."

Mama Helda couldn't hold back any longer and sobbed hysterically. All her defense was gone. Her shoulders shook uncontrollably. Tears streamed between the fingers covering her thin face. She cried for a short while and we let her. Trying to control her sobbing, she told us Pace Poro Boku, had beaten her harder than ever before. He went crazy and repeatedly kicked her pregnant belly. She slowly continued:

"At that moment, I remembered what you told me, Mabel. I have to protect my children. I'm the only one they have. Their father hurts them the way he hurts me. I don't want that. So, I made the decision, Mabel. I took my children and ran away at the break of the dawn. I didn't know where to go. I just wanted to get out of there. But unfortunately, I was too late. He didn't make it, Mabel. It's all my fault. Mine alone."

While they talk, I notice that Mama Helda's belly is flat. The unborn baby, Yosi's youngest brother to-be, is no longer there. She bled while running away, caused by the kicks to her stomach.

The villagers found her unconscious in the middle of a field and took her to the hospital. When she recovered, she chose to stay in this shelter belonging to a church.

"I feel safer here. Content and unafraid. I'll stay for a while, maybe forever. I'm so tired, Mabel. So tired." She cried her heart out in Mabel's arms, and coughed as she cried. It was heartbreaking to watch.

The annoyance Mama Helda once had for Mabel is gone. She longed for love and attention, and Mabel, who regards her as a daughter, can't help but show her a mother's love. Mabel kisses her forehead and teary cheeks while comforting her. The two women hug for a long time, crying about their similar fate.

Maybe this is the right time to tell another story from Mabel's past. She was married to another before Pace Mauwe.

She was close to fifteen years old. After de Wissels left for their home country, Mabel decided to return to her village. She wanted it to be a short visit before she went back to the city to live on her own, but her parents told her to stay. They took her to meet a man who would be her husband if he were willing. The arrangements for the matchmaking started. As it turned out, the ritual offended Mabel as a woman for the first time.

"Pum, I didn't like that man. He looked at me as if I were a thing, not a human. He put a price on me in a disrespectful manner. I'd never been treated like that, but mother said it was the custom. She and the other women here were treated like that when a man wanted to marry them."

She continued in a whisper: "He fondled my breasts with his dark furry hand, Pum. Just like a monkey, checking if the mango he was about to pick was ripe enough. I really hated that guy. I didn't smile at him when he said goodbye. I didn't care. I didn't want to be his wife."

Have you heard the good advice about not to hate someone too much unless you want to bear the consequence? I have, but I forget who told me.

Mabel, who really hated the guy for touching her breasts, had to deal with the fact that he wanted her as a wife. He brought what was for that time an impressive dowry: tens of shells, axes, bows and arrows, and two pigs. That's the equivalent of today's big wedding with live music and inviting the entire village as guests. Her parents were very happy, of course. They decided on the wedding date right away and prepared Mabel to be a bride.

I don't know much about Mabel's husband, other than he was the son of her father's friend and a little older than she. Although he had the appearance of a hunter, big and muscular with dark skin, he looked like an innocent child. He was a contrast from Mabel, who had seen the world from books and meeting people in the city. Nevertheless, they looked good together at the wedding, wearing the traditional Dani tribe's wedding outfit.

Mabel, who was usually full of confidence, changed into a shy bride. She kept her head down most of the time, not even looking at the dashing husband who stood next to her. She had the same attitude when her husband took her to a small cabin in the forest for their honeymoon. Mabel seemed to love her husband more when she returned.

She found out that his hands were not the only furry parts of him. There was another one, and she really liked it. Mabel was sure she would be happy for the rest of her life. And she was happy, but not for long. Five months after the festive wedding, disaster struck.

I get chills every time I recall what she told me.

A big war can start from a small mistake. What happened was small compared to the number of lives lost and the losses to each side. War is a useless competition of egos. Back then the biggest tribal war happened because one tribe kidnapped the woman of another tribe. The woman was Mabel.

One day, men from another tribe kidnapped Mabel as she was cutting sago in the forest. They said she had crossed the border of their village, but everyone knew that was a lie. One kidnapper found Mabel attractive. Maybe it was meant to be.

A tribal war broke out. Although she was returned to her family unharmed, the incident was seen as a disgrace. It hurt what every tribe treasured the most: honor.

The armies of both tribes met on a large field for battle. One tribe felt insulted, the other challenged. Many weapons were wielded to show their strength. Also, the night before, they sent prayers and chants to the spirits of their ancestors asking to grant them victory. They prayed that every arrow took a life and every ax blade chopped off the enemy's head.

That day never goes away. Those screams still trouble Mabel in her sleep. The tension and terror are too real to be only a nightmare. Sometimes she refuses to go back to sleep. That war almost became the last thing she saw in life.

Mabel's father and eldest brother died that day. They died defending the honor of their tribe and Mabel, while her husband acted like a coward. He showed admirable courage on the battlefield, chopping off so many arms, legs, and heads of the enemy. But after the bloodbath, he returned Mabel to her mother and, looking disgusted, asked for his dowry back. He said she was no longer worthy of being a wife of a hero like him.

What a shameless bastard. Unknown to Mabel, I've cursed him in my heart ever since she told me. This is why Mabel and Mama Helda shed the same amount of tears.

"That's how men are, Helda. Their strength and power makes them feel superior. They forget they're only human. The blood shed at their birth and the beads of sweat raising them belong to women."

Outside, the sky is a perfect sapphire blue, according to Mabel. The laughter of Leksi and Yosi fills the air that is getting hotter as the sun climbs higher in the sky.

"We have to stay strong, Helda. Don't give in. We have to keep on fighting for our children and grandchildren. They must have a better life. So be strong, child."

Life as we know it carries on with the wind.

Chapter 11

LEKSI

Independence Day is coming. And pilkada too. I don't know what the word means, it's just that many people have been saying it lately. All I know is there are more flags around. Not just the red and white national flag, but flags of other colors. Some are like the tee shirts Mabel's guests gave us, the ones I gave to Yosi and her brothers.

Speaking of Yosi often makes me sad. I really don't understand why she had to move so far away.

"Do you miss your pace?"

"Nope."

"Why?"

"Because he hurt Mama and he's the reason why my unborn brother is dead."

"That was your pace's fault? I thought he died because your mother delivered him in the middle of the field and not on the bed. That's what Mabel said."

"You're wrong."

"Then?"

"He died because Pace kicked him hard. Like kicking a ball."

"Really? Why didn't you tell me?"

"I'm telling you now. I peeped from behind the bedroom curtain when it happened. My pace is an evil man. I'm not going back home. I'm afraid he will kick me or my other brothers to death."

I can't persuade Yosi to come home. She enjoys living in her new place together with many other people. But she admits she doesn't think she can find another best friend like me there. Of course, I like hearing this. But I'm also sad because we can't meet as often as we used to. We can only meet when Mabel has the time to take me there on weekends.

From now on, I have to play alone. Pum is too busy admiring the colorful flags and banners lining the road of our village. Kwee is always there for me, but I can't ask him to play jumping rope let alone pretend to cook. He only likes playing tag and I'm tired of that game.

Karel shows up in my front yard. It has been a while since the last time I played with him. He looks taller and wears new clothes. I mean, I never saw him in them when we played together. The last time I saw him ended very badly. He insulted Mabel and she got angry.

I don't remember what he said about her, but she spent the entire day grumbling. She even cursed Pace Gerson, Karel's father.

"Are Mabel and Pace Gerson enemies?" I ask Mace.

"Says who?"

"I heard her curse him. I also noticed how they never say hello when they meet in the street."

"But they smile at each other, right?"

"Well, yes."

"There you go. You're wrong then."

"No, it's not me. I heard someone said that."

"Who?"

"People."

"Leksi, have you been eavesdropping again?"

"No, no. I wouldn't dare."

"Fine, let me tell you something. Listen to me. Mabel and Pace Gerson are not enemies. Your Mabel doesn't like his attitude, that's all. And that's why she doesn't feel like saying hello when they see each other."

"What attitude?"

"You don't need to know that."

"But I want to know."

Then Mace said that Pace Gerson often annoyed Mabel.

"Annoyed by what?"

"Things that make her not like him. Have you ever felt like that about one of your friends?"

I really don't understand what Mace said. Maybe Pace Gerson has the same annoying traits as Karel who was boastful and selfish.

I don't like playing with Karel. Not because he's older than I am, but because his bad attitude annoys me. But he always has interesting new toys that grab my attention.

He is the first kid in the village to own a bicycle. He also has battery-powered cars and robots, a light-up sword, and a *gim boy*—that's what he calls a little box that produces sounds and a picture that moves by pushing buttons.

Karel made the kids in our village crazy about badminton. Holding his racket—one that looked like those used by real athletes on the television at the coop office—Karel turned the street into a badminton court. He made the other kids cry with envy at the caped clothes he wears while playing.

When he suddenly shows up, I wonder what kind of toys he will brag about this time. But he doesn't bring anything new, just two ordinary tires. He lends one to me and challenges me to a race. I play with him.

Karel knows what pilkada means. I ask him about it while siting on his bike, and he explains it to me. He says he heard everything from his father.

"How does your pace know?"

"Because he's smart. Besides, he and one of the candidates for regent position are good friends."

"Friends you say?"

"Yes. That man came to my house a couple of times. His car is very nice. The windows have curtains like those in a house. He has a couple of tough-looking escorts who follow him everywhere."

"Why? Does he trip a lot when walking? Is that why he has to be escorted?"

"Silly little girl. Escorts are protectors, Leksi, bodyguards. They protect him in case a bad guy wants to hurt him."

"Oh I see. Does your pace have bodyguards too?"

"Not for now. Maybe when he runs for the pilkada next year."

"Pace Gerson is so cool. Why doesn't he run now? I want to see the bodyguards, Karel."

"He doesn't have enough money. He's still saving."

"Money? For what?"

"To be the candidate for regent."

"Oh, so that takes money. I thought only school takes money. Then how does he do it?"

"Do what?"

"How does your pace get all that money?"

Instead of replying, Karel rings his bell and pedals away.

I gave it a rest. My question was so stupid that he stayed quiet.

That night, I tell Mabel and Mace about my conversation with Karel. I don't expect Mabel's harsh response.

"For sure, Leksi, he'll get the money by selling his ancestors' land and even his honor. That's what Gerson does. He's a shameless Papuan with an ambition to be a regent. What a power thirsty ass-licker."

***

145

The sun comes up and chases the night away for the new day to begin. I'm walking home from school when I run into Karel riding his bike. He says he is coming to my house to pick me up and take me to his house. Someone wants to see me, he says.

"Who?" I ask.

Karel only shrugs. Being very curious, this makes me even more curious. So, I walk to his house instead of going straight home.

"I hope you have food. I'm starving."

"Don't worry. You won't regret this."

Karel's house looks like it's always ready to welcome guests. Jars and jars of cookies, peanuts, and crackers are on the living room table. My mouth waters when I see them from the front door. Karel's mother gives me a very warm welcome and seems to know I'm hungry. "Help yourself. Don't be shy."

In minutes, I have snacks in my stomach. I completely enjoy myself because Karel's mother leaves the room after she opens the jars. Freedom. My hand moves in and out of the jars. I don't stop until a man with a neat haircut enters from behind the curtain, together with Karel's mother who brings me a drink.

The person who wants to see me is Karel's father, Pace Gerson. The big man with glasses is as friendly as his wife. He laughs a lot and tells hilarious new *mops*. My jaw and stomach hurt from laughing at his jokes. For a second, I envy Karel. He's so lucky. Not many paces like to joke. We have a lot more drunken and violent paces. When we

146

are done laughing, he asks me about my school, Mace, and Mabel.

"May God always grant her good health and strength," he says when I say Mabel looks tired these recent days. What he says makes me start blaming Mabel. She is wrong about Karel's father. He's been nothing but fun, caring, and kind. Look at the presents he gives me: three tee shirts, posters, and stickers.

"Mabel never got these ones."

"Really?" He sounds surprised.

"Only those from Striped Party, Flowery Party, and…"

I try to remember the name, but Pace Gerson interrupts me. "Ah, never mind. I know all those parties." He waves his giant hand, the one with a huge gold ring, in front of his round nose as if he were shooing a fly.

As I watch him, I catch a look that says he's better than me. Karel often has the same look. I shouldn't have told him the things I did.

"Umm, but she doesn't have any of them. I gave some to Yosi." I say, hoping to please Pace Gerson sitting in front of me. I really don't want to offend him. Mace and Mabel always remind me to mind my manners when I visit someone's house. Then Karel says something that almost makes me stop being a well-mannered girl.

"Who? Yosi the stinky kid?" Karel snickers and pinches his nose. He sits on my right and I can see him out of the corner of my eyes.

I growl in protest. Karel seems to forget that Yosi is my best friend and I don't like anyone mocking her. Besides,

147

maybe there's something wrong with his nose because he smells bad himself.

"Karel, stop it, or do you want me to hit you?" Pace Gerson snarls so quickly that it surprises me.

I almost kick Karel's foot but I change my mind. I thought that with all the jokes Pace Gerson tells me, he never gets angry. But I'm wrong. He certainly does. Scared, I glance at his face. I want to see his angry face. Is it like Pace Poro Boku's?

There's a big change in his face. The friendliness he showed earlier is gone, only this creepy, angry look. His eyebrows arch so high, they look like they will dash away any second and leave only his bulging eyes. I hold back my shudder. Pace Gerson is really scary. I want to get out of there right away, but what about Karel?

He hangs his head in fear, like sunrays are coming out of his father's eyes, too powerful to resist. I smile, relieved. Karel will not dare insult Yosi again. I'm even gladder when I see Pace Gerson smile again. He smiles just for me, I know.

When we continue our chat, Pace Gerson starts to talk about the parties. "Leksi, you are just a kid, that's true. But let me tell you, those parties you mentioned earlier are cheap. They're different from my party, kid. Mine is the classiest." He points at a giant brown poster on the living room wall, right next to the bedroom door. "The People's Soul Mate Party." He reads aloud the big letters printed in bold at the bottom of the poster, below the picture of a dancing fish.

"Let me explain, kid. Our party is invincible. The brown color means we're like the earth, always ready to support the people. Fertile earth gives a better life. The picture of a fish means that our country is made of islands and surrounded by the sea." He sounds so confident that I'm stunned at his explanation.

Before I can stop myself, I blurt out, "I've never seen the sea, Pace Gerson. Have you?"

He chuckles as if he doesn't expect the question. But he quickly goes back to being confident and says he has seen the sea.

Unfortunately, Karel right away contradicts him.

Pace Gerson raises his eyebrows again. This time he shows his anger through a loud snort like an angry swine. Our conversation ends right there. He orders Karel to take me home. "Don't make her Mabel and Mace worried," he says firmly before being friendly again, "Come back three days before Independence Day, Leksi, and I'll have Karel pick you up. Our party holds many competitions in the celebration.

"There'll be a chip-eating and needle-threading competition, sack racing, and many other games. You'd like that, wouldn't you?

"Just so you know, we'll have great prizes: bicycles, televisions, gas stoves, radios, and a scooter. You can bring Mabel, Mace, all your neighbors, and everyone else you know. Even everyone at the market. The more the merrier. Don't forget, kid."

On the way home, sitting at the back of Karel's squeaking bike, I try to imagine Mabel's face when she learns that Pace Gerson is actually kind. Would she like him and let me go to his house for the competitions? I hope so, as I really want to win a bike. I would love to ride it to school or to Yosi's. I can't wait.

PUM

For the first time since the incident, Mabel smiles again. She tries hard to keep her tired eyes open to finish the last noken. She's done weaving it. All she needs to do is tidy up the knots and threads before putting it inside a big plastic bag, with the rest of the nokens. With that done, she waits for the client to pick them up and pay her a good sum of money for the hard work. She hasn't had enough sleep for a week and took a break from selling pinang to finish on time. This is how Mabel got the noken order:

"Just make as many nokens as you can to sell at the Cultural Exhibition from the 16th to 18th," says Mama Mote. "I also gave this job to other mamas in another district. My boss has a lot of money and wants to join the exhibition. He just doesn't have any idea regarding what to enter with. He'll pay a lot because he thinks he'll make a lot. What do you say, Mabel? Will you take the job?"

"My, my, Mama Mote. Apparently, you're rich now. You have an employer able to spread some money around."

Mama Mote comes to Mabel's pinang stall on the sidewalk. She hands out brochures about the Cultural Exhibition, and wants Mabel to fill a big order.

"Just think, business is hard these days. The petatas seller with the most customers can only make twenty or thirty thousand rupiah a day. Pinang sellers make even less. Unless you carry your goods, you have to spend money for transportation."

She says Mabel will earn a few hundred thousand rupiah.

"Make small nokens. People like those better because they can use them for their wallet, pinang, and small telephone if they have one."

If Mabel agrees, she will give her the materials that day, and then Mabel can start weaving at home.

"A good noken is made out of tree bark or sago boughs, not yarn, Mama Mote. Yarn breaks too easily. No good."

"Oh, Mabel, you're so behind the times. Who buys a noken made of bark these days? Young people prefer the ones made of yarn. Besides, it takes too long to make the bark kind. We don't have enough time, Mabel."

Mama Mote has the reputation of being persuasive. Her affect on Mabel is no exception. After Mama Mote leaves to buy the materials, Mabel whispers to me that if the job works out, she will fulfill her promise to Leksi.

"I promised her a chicken dinner, but I couldn't when the company failed to buy my vegetables. I feel bad for her. She can only watch the immigrants enjoy good food at the stalls in the market."

A few moments later Mabel receives a couple of plastic bags filled with yarn to make nokens.

"Why only two colors? Do you want them like the flag?"

"Yes. Weave nokens in the colors of our flag, red and white. Independence Day is coming soon. The people who buy these nokens, especially the youth, will remember the flag of their country."

Mabel counts the number of yarn skeins and estimates the number of nokens she can make from them. Mama Mote has too much white yarn.

"There's not enough red yarn. What shall I do? Make them all white or...."

"No, no. I'll buy more. Wait here." Mama Mote heads back to the market and returns in a pedicab with a bag of yarn. "Someone bought all the red," she said when Mabel protests. "Just use this blue, Mabel. So the nokens will be blue and white."

"But it's green, Mama Mote, not blue."

"Green? Fine. Whatever you say," she said, laughing.

This bothers me. What is Mama Mote up to?

"The only thing to worry about is I'm coming next week to pick up the order. I'll pay you on that day. Cash."

Mama Mote's laughter makes me very ill at ease. I watch as she says goodbye in an overly friendly way and gets back in the pedicab. I don't notice anything suspicious.

Mama Mote is an expert in weaving a lie into the believable. One must always be careful with her. But I don't sense she had lied. The information about the

Cultural Exhibition is everywhere, even on a giant banner. She told Mabel the truth about it. As for the noken order, I know that buying the yarn and paying a pedicab for such a short distance are not done to trick Mabel into making nokens for her. If she refuses to pay, Mabel won't give her the nokens. Fair and square.

I shook off my bad premonition. Or I hoped it wouldn't turn out as bad as what happened three days before:

We harvested petatas and rica that day. Mabel takes a rest from selling pinang on the sidewalk to help Mace in the market. She also takes me, Leksi, and Kwee, who is very excited, with her. A special guest happens to visit the market. People say a man running for regent will hold a campaign rally. Others say he will buy everything without haggling. So, the market is far busier and crowded than usual—and this is when I start to feel bad. The maces who sell vegetables put on makeup to attract attention, while the butchers wash with soap to shake hands with the candidate. Mabel does not allow Mace to act like them.

"There are very few good and honest people these days, Lisbeth, especially among the rich and those have power. Beware if they are good to you. Just wait and you'll see how soon they ask you to repay them. When that happens, they'll be your master whether you like it or not."

Before noon, the waiting crowd moves into the narrow and muddy aisle of the market. Almost everyone in the market gathers around a group of slow-walking paces that wear brown tee shirts with a picture of dancing fish.

"That's the People's Soul Mate Party," exclaims Leksi, who turns out to know the candidate's party. "Pace Gerson's party. He must be here. I want to see him," she says enthusiastically.

Leksi's excitement is squelched by Mabel's loud voice. "Don't go anywhere, Leksi. Stay put."

I've never heard Mabel talk like this to her granddaughter, who doesn't expect it either. The little girl hides under the stall table, away from Mabel's anger. Mace, who is arranging the petatas nearby, only throws a meaningful look. Only she and I understand how angry Mabel can be when she hears the mention of Pace Gerson.

Leksi came home a little late from school and said she had been at Pace Gerson's house. She innocently told us everything, and handed Mabel three brown tee shirts, one poster, and many stickers.

"For Mace and Mabel," she said, before letting them know they were invited to join the Independence Day celebration games at Pace Gerson's place.

"I want to join every competition if I can. He said there'll be a bike as a prize and I really want one."

Mabel was furious. And she is furious again when the group from People's Soul Mate Party stops in front of her stall. They yell out what they will do if they win the election. This includes providing free school, free medical care at the hospital, a housing complex, and even stoves.

"We'd provide this out of our concern. We care about the common people who are often oppressed and victimized. Don't forget to vote for us at the election.

Number four. Just remember number four. We're the only party that cares."

The crowd goes wild, like endless roar of applause and compliments are about to burst through the plastic tarps hung low over the heads of the vegetable sellers. A familiar female voice interrupts the noise.

Complete silence takes over. It's like someone told the crowd to leave. All eyes are on an old woman who stands defiant with disgust on her face.

Mabel addresses the campaigners fearlessly. "Tsk. Another lie. Do you think we're that gullible?" She goes on, "You keep making promises but never keep any of them. Your promises are like the spit coming out of your mouth. Once it leaves your mouth, you forget it's yours.

"As a candidate, you should be ashamed. You should also be ashamed for receiving this warm welcome from sweaty peddlers who have been working very hard since morning. You only come here when you need our vote. When you're not looking for votes, you prefer to frequent the clean and non-smelly market. The market for the rich. You wouldn't want to come to this kind of market, let alone shake the smelly hands of the fishmongers or smile back at the vegetable sellers. Do you play us for fools, ignorant of these facts?"

What happened that afternoon gave Mabel a somber look, making her look older. Although many people at the market agree, some curse at her. Since that day, she's been the object of their conversation and criticism. Some do it secretly, some say it in the open. Mabel is quite taken aback and sad that people don't understand her good intentions.

"I just want them to see those officials' true colors, Pum. Why do they treat me like an enemy? What do I benefit from all this? Nothing, right? I'm so sad. They're ignorant and refuse to learn."

Mabel spends a lot of time wondering how she has wronged the market people and about that damned pilkada. If the noken order can make her smile again, it surely makes me happy and the same goes for Leksi.

The girl feels guilty for what happened after Mabel's comment to the candidates.

Pace Gerson comes to Mabel's stall with a group of muscular men. They are paid thugs, and everybody knows except Leksi. Pace Gerson chides Mabel, who responds with harsh words. He finally walks away, leaving Mabel with a threat.

"Let him be, Pum. Don't." She stops me from chasing Pace Gerson and teaching him a lesson. "A threat is just a threat for we have no power over fate. Even if I die today, it won't be because of that ass-licker, but because it is my time. Don't be afraid."

She is right. She's still alive, happily working on her noken order while Leksi keeps her company.

"You know, child, since our ancestors' time, every woman of our land must be able to make a noken. A good and strong noken means more fertility and prosperity for her tribe. When you can't make one, it means you're not grown up or ready to get married."

"Oh really? I'm bored watching you make the noken. Can I can go out and play for a little while? I'm still a kid anyway."

"You're always good at finding excuses. I'll teach you how to make a noken one day because you're a Komen girl. I don't want you to turn into one of those women who are only smart but forget about their traditions."

This is the last thing I hear Mabel say before loud banging on the door alerts me.

"What's with Mama Mote? Why was she so impatient? Didn't she say she would pick up the order late in the afternoon?"

Chapter 12

KWEE

With just a bit of psychic ability to see the future, I would do something for sure. But what can I do now? I can't even yell for help. They arrest Mabel in front of me.

Poor Mabel.

Mama Kori's story came to life, and it is even scarier when I witness it. It really happens.

Once more, big and muscular men arrest Mabel. Some of them carry a rifle. They are truly violent and cruel. They have no manners, just like Mama Kori said. They bang on our door before breaking it open and storming in. Like a tiger eyeing its prey, they circle Mabel as she sits on a screw-pines mat at work on the nokens. One man grabs the last noken from her wrinkly hand and throws it to the ground while accusing her of making the enemy's flag.

"It's a noken, child, not a flag."

"Shut up. Everybody knows that."

"So what's the problem?"

"Don't try making excuses. You intentionally make them in the color of the flag, don't you?"

"That's right. Red and white."

"Liar. Look, some are blue and white. These colors represent the enemy's flag. You will soon add a picture of the sun for sure."

"You're wrong, child. There's no picture of any sun. There are only two kinds of nokens. One is red and white and the other green and white. Just what Mama Mote requested."

"Green you say? This is blue, Mama."

"It's green."

"Blue."

"Green, child."

"Blue, I say. Take a good look. Or are you color blind, huh?"

My goodness. I'm miserable when they start to ruin the stack of nokens with the muzzle of their rifles. Mabel had arranged the nokens neatly in a plastic bag. But my sadness quickly turns to anger when a man with severe bloodshot eyes throws those nokens into Mabel's face.

Leksi cries, "No, don't ruin them. Don't."

"Please treat her nicely, sir. She's old. Please," Mace pleads.

"I've done nothing wrong. You're mistaken. I made these according to the order. I didn't have a say in the colors. Just ask Mama Mote. She knows everything."

Mama Kori had the perfect description for them: heartless. Leksi's cry, Mace's plea, and Mabel's defense have no effect on them. The violent men keep pushing Mabel to admit that she was wrong and they don't think twice about ruining the chairs, closets, tables, almost everything in the room. I hear them throw everything in the kitchen across the room.

While this is going on, Pum and I stand by the three miserable members of our family—Mabel, Mace, and Leksi. We try to stop the barbaric men, but it's useless. They are far stronger than us. They kick Pum in the head until he collapses. I'm knocked down for a while by kicks to my stomach.

What makes me furious are the neighbors and people gathered in front of our house. It hurts to see that no one has the courage to save our family. I have no doubt they could do it.

Pace Gerson is among them. I know that if wants to help, he can use his power to order the heartless men to treat Mabel well. But he and the rest of them only watch and whisper to one another. They witness every minute of the men forcing Mabel to leave the house and step on her hand as she clings to the porch steps, right to when they brutally shove the old woman into a car.

"Don't cry, Lisbeth. Be a strong woman for me. And Leksi, promise me to study well. Don't be color blind like your Mabel so you won't be easily tricked. And don't turn your heart into stone like those who tricked and hurt us. Take care. I'll be home soon."

I know what having a nightmare means. A nightmare is finding yourself in the middle of a reality without a place to hide or an escape from its ugliness. And my family is experiencing a nightmare.

***

No one sleeps tonight. We stay awake although yawns escape from our mouths many times. We are thinking about Mabel, and guess what she has to face in that hell on earth. Is she experiencing the same horrors as she had back then?

"I'm sure she's fine, Leksi. You just go to sleep," Mace whispered to Leksi who kept on calling Mabel's name. But the sad look in Mace's eyes betrayed her words.

Without a doubt, this is the hardest day for us, especially Mabel and Mace. On top of today's incident, Mace also has to face her fear of armed men. That was why she could only look on helplessly when they dragged Mabel out of the house. Unlike Leksi, she was too afraid to grab those men's arms and legs. She couldn't bring herself to look at their faces. Mace had seen the heavy black boots before, when their owners took turns violating her body savagely. That's how she got the agony that showed on her face at noon, like the same glass shard from her past cut her heart open once again. She was horrified.

My mother knew what had happened. This is what she told me:

We lived in a small village by the forest. It was peaceful, far from city noise or any other upheaval. We thought the peace would last. And it did until the armed men appeared out of nowhere. We admired their stiff posture, but that feeling turned into hatred and fear when we learned how cruel they were.

Everyone in the village knows the chaos started when they came. Anyone who says they were there to protect our village is telling a lie. They brought chaos. We had no more peace in the village because it felt as if someone was always watching. They created so many rules and bans, and punishment waited for those who broke them. They treated the entire village and the crops, land, houses, and even the food in our kitchens as if it were theirs. They were cunning and swift like rats you couldn't stop from sharing your home and food.

They always had a reason to drag a villager to their place. No one was brave enough to refuse, or had the courage to fight them. They treated us like doormats in our own homes. The stupidest thing was we didn't do anything about it.

At that time, Mace and Pace Johanis was a young couple with one child, Lukas. Mace was fifteen while Pace Johanis was four or five years older. They seemed happy although they only lived from their harvest and hunting. But after Lukas was born, Pace Johanis changed. He decided to look for a job in the city, leaving Mace and Lukas in the village. Then the disaster happened.

In the early evening, Lisbeth and I were on our way from our field at the outskirts of the village. We went home later than usual because fruit needed harvesting. She trudged with a heavy load on her back. Other than Lukas, petatas and jackfruit were stuffed in her noken. But Lisbeth seemed very happy. She sang as she walked. She told me she would sell some of the harvest to get some extra money and buy something for little Lukas.

She stopped singing when three armed men walked toward us. They had just left the village. At first, they walked in silence. We only heard the heavy footsteps of their black boots. When they spotted Lisbeth, who stood aside to make way for them, they began to laugh.

They approached the young and sweet Lisbeth. They flirted with her but she said nothing. She stayed quiet even when their filthy hands touched her face and arm. Then they saw what was inside her noken: the sleeping Lukas. They laughed aloud.

I don't know what demon possessed them. The three good-looking men turned into three bastards. They dragged Lisbeth into a field and raped her. They didn't care when the poor girl kissed their boots and begged them to stop, just like they ignored Lukas, who woke and started to cry.

Of course, I fought my best. But I couldn't do anything after a rifle hit me hard in the head.

That incident made Mace scared of armed men with heavy black boots. Barbaric men who destroyed her life and dreams.

Pace Johanis returned to the village and was furious when he found out. But his fury was not at the rapists, it was at Mace. He often cursed her, even in front of Lukas. He called her whore, slut, and many other insulting names. She was the victim of her husband's fury. To him, she was nothing but a filthy and unworthy woman. He shouted that he wanted to end their marriage, and then left, saying he would never come back. That never happened. He returned a few times to see her and Lukas, and the visits never ended well. He drank a lot at the stall and came home completely wasted. He then beat his wife who had waited up for him and semi-consciously had sex with her. This happened for some time until she told him she was pregnant. He swore he couldn't be the father. It had to be another man. He left and never came back. She decided to look for him in the city.

Pum's faint barks interrupt my musing. *Kwee, go to sleep. I'll be on guard.*

I look for him and there he is. The old chap is sitting in front of the door. Fully alert, he acts tough, as if he's still young.

No way. You go to sleep.

Don't argue, Kwee.

Who's arguing?

You, smart-ass little pig.

Well, then you're a phony. An old dog pretending to be tough.

Pum lets out an angry growl. I refuse to back down, so I do too.

"Pum, Kwee, please don't fight this late. Leksi just fell asleep. You'll wake her."

Only one pair of eyes goes to sleep this night. They are not mine.

Chapter 13

PUM

We can only count on me, not anyone else. Yes, me. Mace is still afraid of armed men, so it's not right to ask her to look for Mabel. Judging by the horror on her face, I thought she would pass out during Mabel's arrest. She trembled badly as she tried to hold back the furious Leksi who wouldn't let those men take her Mabel away.

Luckily, Mace can still function. I know for sure the heavy blow left her shaky, but she gives it her all to hold on. She tries to act as if everything is fine, ignoring the neighbors' whispers. She patiently comforts Leksi who cried all night and day. She works in the field although I see her occasionally stop to cry. I find Mace's behavior impressive. She is indeed a strong woman and has to stay strong, just as Mabel told her before the men carried her away.

Maybe Kwee noticed that for these past two days, I've been on guard and suspicious of everyone without exception. Mabel has enemies out there who would love to see her suffer. One of them is Pace Gerson, I'm sure. That ass-licker watched from across the yard when Mabel was dragged out of the house. He stood in the front row and was ready to watch before the rest of the crowd showed up. Although there's no sign of Mama Mote, I'm sure the gossip queen works for Pace Gerson. Both of them worked together to bring Mabel down for the same reason. Mabel loves to comment harshly about them. Pace Gerson is an ass-licker ready to give up his honor for wealth and power, and Mama Mote never stops spreading lies.

Mabel hates Pace Gerson more than Mama Mote. Although she knows that almost every bad rumor about her starts from Mama Mote lips, she's still friendly to her. But she never greets Pace Gerson.

Mabel welcomed Mama Mote in her house during the tribal war some time ago. Just recently, she accepted the noken order that harmed her. Did Pace Gerson talk Mama Mote into helping him hurt her? In a hard time like this, money can buy anything.

This is the third day since they took Mabel away. There hasn't been any news at all. Kind people are brave enough to knock on our door while others are too afraid to come close. They stop by for a minute or two, and check up on Mace and Leksi and bring us food. They wish and pray that Mabel is fine and will soon be home. But that's not what I want to hear. I need to know for sure she's still alive, and whether she's missing any body parts. It's impossible that they would set her free unharmed.

The squash seller, Mabel's friend at the market, came last night with two giant squashes. "Maybe she'll be lucky enough to return soon."

"But she's innocent," argued Mace.

"Let's pray to Jesus for a miracle that will touch the hearts of those men. They're still human."

Yes, heartless humans, I answered. We saw how cruel they can be. They stepped on Mabel's hand when she tried to hold on to the porch steps. I felt her suffering when the painful scream escaped her mouth. That's why I decide to look for her this morning when everyone in the house is still asleep, except for Kwee.

Do you know the place? Kwee asks. Lately, he seems to be cutting down on his sleep. Is he thinking about Mabel? He's pretty unpredictable.

I sadly shake my head. *I don't. Just guessing.*

So where?

Where what?

Is the place you're guessing?

I wonder for a moment whether I can trust the young Kwee. Will he do something stupid if I tell him the location? He seems to understand my silence.

I promise I won't follow you. I'll stay on guard here. I'll keep Leksi company.

All right then. You gave me your word, so now you have to keep it."

The wind carries the information I whisper to Kwee.

***

The yard is hidden by lush bushes and surrounded by wire fence that is getting rusty. Many people stand around a small podium that appears holy with its fresh white paint. Three tall men guard an equally tall worship pole nearby. The men are not armed, unlike those around the wire fence. The wire fence men hold many kinds of weapons to give them the sense of power and authority.

Did they use those weapons to hurt Mabel? Did they hit her in the head or in the belly?

The thought fuels my anger and desire to find her. I use my snout to part the bush a little. All kinds of smells rush through and I see a line of people with hair as big as the bushes. I know their scent. It is the scent of our people.

Where does Mabel stand? Does she face west, east, north, or south?

I move my head sniffing, and use my eyes as well. I check the yard until a noise like an angry buzzing bee grabs my attention. The worship pole guards stiffly move forward in rhythm, like the toy robots Karel showed Leksi.

What is happening? Do the people who arrested Mabel belong to some strange, secret cult, like the headhunters who worship dead people's heads? I once saw that tribe perform a similar sacred ritual. They chanted mantras that gave me goose bumps right in front of their object of worship. Since when did Mabel become an enemy of those savages?

In the middle of my confusion, the breeze carries a familiar scent to my nostrils. I see Mabel standing in the line over there. I know it's her when I hear her scream, and I inhale the scent of her breath, which is so close to mine I'd pick it up from any distance.

Oh no. What have they done to you, Mabel?

I jump from my hiding place and run through the bushes. I push my nose through an opening in the wire and press my face against the fence to get a better look. My Mabel cringes in pain. Her right arm is swollen. Has a guard harmed her arm and made her scream?

I don't need to guess for long. A man swings a bat at the back of her knees. She screams again. Louder this time.

Damn it, I have to do something. I will not allow them to mistreat an old woman.

I ram the fence. I can get through because it's not securely fastened. I hit it again. I almost succeed when men start running toward me. I know this too late because my nostrils are filled with Mabel's scent. Each of them carries a weapon.

Swoosh! Thud!

A big rock hits me.

Swoosh! Thud!

Another one hits me in the head.

This is the end for me. I feel the presence of my old friend, Death.

"Quick, kill that dog."

There he is. Friendly as usual. But why doesn't he come closer?

Ssh, Pum. I'm here. Behind the tree. Pum.

Kwee?

Yes. It's me. I'm sorry I broke my promise. Leksi made me. She wouldn't stop crying because she couldn't find you. Pum, she's afraid of losing you and so am I. Let's get out of here. Come on.

But my head is hurt, Kwee.

Don't worry, I'll help you.

Oh, Kwee. I don't want to lose you either. Maybe I've been too hard on you all this time, but I had a reason. I wanted to make you braver and more active. We're different, yes, but we're one family. You, Mabel, Mace, Leksi, and me.

I look lovingly at Kwee, who pushes me with all his might. But it doesn't work. He looks very worried. But I'm not. I feel Death coming closer and closer, as close as my own kidney or brain.

You go, Kwee. Take good care of Leksi and Mace.

No, I won't leave without you.

Please, don't argue. And don't cry. They're coming.

Thump-thump-thump.

"Hunt that pig too. The one by the tree."

"We'll have a feast all night long. Ha-ha!"

Kwee. They're going to catch you. Run, Kwee, run.

Bash! Bam!

Bash! Bam!

Woof! Woof!

Oink! Oink!

Notes

Chapter 1

Purple-stemmed *keris* plant: *Alocasia lauterbachiana*, also known as Baroque sword, native to Papua and believed to have superior healing power.

Yellow-finned *arowana*: Fresh water fish, also known as Paradise fish.

Pinang: Mixture of areca nut, betel leaf, and gambir, made from the twigs and leaves of *Uncaria gambir*, a tropical vine.

Paitua: Local dialect for husband.

Mace: Pronounced "ma-che," local dialect for mother.

Sago palm: *Metroxylon sagu*, or true sago palm, a major food resource for Papua.

Karaka: Local dialect for mud crab.

Komen: Local dialect for native Papuans, as opposed to immigrants.

Pak: Respectful term of address for an older man, meaning "father."

Pace: Pronounced "pa-che," local dialect for father.

Chapter 2

Bakar batu: Meat, sweet potato, and banana are wrapped in banana leaves and cooked in an earth pit lined with hot stones, a feast for important events like harvests and births.

Chapter 3

Tomi-tomi: A cheap alcoholic beverage made from grain. The brand is *Topi Miring*, from *topi*, meaning hat, and *miring*, meaning slanted.

Chapter 4

Petatas: Local dialect for sweet potatoes.

Chapter 5

Rica: Local dialect for Bird's Eye chilies, ranked 100,000–225,000 on the Scoville scale.

Kangkung: Local dialect for *Ipomoea aquatic*, also known as water spinach.

Ayam kampong: Free-range indigenous chicken.

Meno: Local dialect for addressing a native Papuan, meaning brother.

Chapter 6

Koteka: Penis sheath made from a gourd that identifies the wearer with specific tribe. Small ones are worn for everyday use, while larger and decorated kotekas are worn for festivals.

Sally: Traditional Papuan skirt made from woven orchid fibers.

Pengayau: Indonesian for headhunter.

Ots: Money in the form of shells broken into flakes with bored holes and threaded on fibers.

Chayote: Squash with flat round seed in the center, also known as pear squash and vegetable pear.

Chapter 7

Galangal: Native root with flowery flavor used in Indonesian cooking.

Chapter 8

Karet Merdeka: Traditional jumping game using a rope made of rubber bands stitched together. The goal of game is to let each of player jump over the rope without using their hands. When a player completes a jump, the height of the rope increases until it is stretched above the head. A player will shout "*merdeka*," meaning free or independence in Indonesian, when the last jump is completed.

Chapter 9
Poro Boku: Local dialect for "big belly."
Roda Gelinding: A game of pushing a bicycle wheel forward using a short stick.

Chapter 10
Pilkada: Regional elections.

Chapter 11
Mops: Jokes told among Papuans, from the Dutch word, "mop."

About the Author

Award-winning author Anindita Siswanto Thayf was born in Makassar and has loved words since her youth, writing short stories through her high school years. Some of these were published in the local newspaper, Pedoman Rakyat. In 2001, to satisfy her father's wishes, she obtained a degree in Electrical Engineering from the Hassanudin University in Makassar.

Unable to secure employment as an electrical engineer, Anindita wrote feature articles and was assistant editor for Majalah Makassar Terkini. Local as well as national media have published her essays and short stories. Her novel, Tanah Tabu (GagasMedia, 2013), won the 2008 Jakarta Arts Council Novel Competition. Other award-winning works include Jejak Kala (Penerbit Andi, 2009) won the 2010 Award for Indonesian Literature and Language from the Yogyakarta Council on Language. "Lagu Sup Jagung" placed second in the 2010 Short Story Competition of Majalah Femina. Her novel, Ulin, took first prize in the 2012 Serial Novel Competition of Majalah Femina.

Anindita is currently a full-time writer and at work on another historical novel. She and her husband, Ragil, live on the slope of Mount Merapi, surrounded by salak plantations.

More Storytellers from Dalang Publishing

Only a Girl
Lian Gouw

Three generations of Chinese women struggle for identity against a political backdrop of the World Depression, World War II, and the Indonesian Revolution. Nanna, the matriarch of the family, strives to preserve the family's traditional Chinese values while her children are eager to assimilate into Dutch colonial society. Carolien, Nanna's youngest daughter, is fixated on the advantages to be gained by adopting a western lifestyle. Jenny's western upbringing puts her at a disadvantage in the new independent Indonesian, where Dutch culture is no longer revered. The unique ways in which Nanna, Carolien, and Jenny face their own challenges reveal the complexity of Chinese society in Indonesia between 1930 and 1952.

Price: $17.95
Paperback: 298 pages
ISBN: 978-0-9836273-7-1

My Name is Mata Hari
Remy Sylado
Translated from the Indonesian by Dewi Anggraeni

My Name is Mata Hari tells the story of Margaretha Geertruida Zelle, a young Dutch woman married to an older military officer assigned to the Dutch East Indies. Claiming her mother's Javanese ancestry, she changed her name to Mata Hari, Malay for "eye of the day."

As Mata Hari, she danced on stages across Europe and the Middle East, and took many high-ranking military and government officials as her lovers. Convicted of espionage during World War I, she said at the end of her tumultuous life, "I am a genuine courtesan. And I am a dancer in the true sense."

Price: $17.95
Paperback: 334 pages
ISBN: 978-0-9836273-0-2

***

Potions and Paper Cranes
Lan Fang
Translated from the Indonesian by Elisabet Titik Murtisari

In Lan Fang's award-winning novel, Sulis is a young woman selling potions in Surabaya's harbor district. She meets Sujono, a day laborer with dreams of becoming a freedom fighter, and whose passion for Matsumi, a geisha called to Java by a Japanese general, is destined to ruin all of them. Each tells the story of their lives during the Japanese occupation of Java and Indonesia's transition from a Dutch colony to an independent republic.

Price: $17.95
Paperback: 252 pages
ISBN: 978-0-9836273-3-3

Kei
Erni Aladjai
Translated from the Indonesian by Nurhayat Indriyatno Mohamed

At the end of Suharto's New Order, the Kei people hold on to their traditions as they flee the violence that divides Muslim from Christian and destroys the villages. Namira, a Muslim girl, works as a volunteer in a refugee camp when she meets Sala, a young Protestant man. Grounded in the islander's belief of "We drink from the same spring and eat from the same land, the land of Kei," the two fall in love amid the chaos that will soon separate them.

Price: $17.95
Paperback: 226 pages
ISBN: 978-0-9836273-6-4

CPSIA information can be obtained
at www.ICGtesting.com
Printed in the USA
FSOW02n2003281014
3334FS

6 · 19